SISTER, MISSING

Award-winning books from Sophie McKenzie

GIRL, MISSING
Winner Richard and Judy Best Kids' Books 2007 12+
Winner of the Red House Children's Book Award 2007 12+
Winner of the Manchester Children's Book Award 2008
Winner of the Bolton Children's Book Award 2007
Winner of the Grampian Children's Book Award 2008
Winner of the John Lewis Solihull Book Award 2008
Winner of the Lewisham Children's Book Award
Winner of the 2008 Sakura Medal

SIX STEPS TO A GIRL
Winner of the Manchester Children's Book Award 2009

BLOOD TIES
Overall winner of the Red House Children's Book Award 2009
Winner of the Leeds Book Award 2009 age 11–14 category
Winner of the Spellbinding Award 2009
Winner of the Lancashire Children's Book Award 2009
Winner of the Portsmouth Book Award 2009 (Longer Novel section)
Winner of the Staffordshire Children's Book Award 2009
Winner of the Southern Schools Book Award 2010
Winner of the RED Book Award 2010
Winner of the Warwickshire Secondary Book Award 2010
Winner of the Grampian Children's Book Award 2010
Winner of the North East Teenage Book Award 2010

THE MEDUSA PROJECT: THE SET-UP
Winner of the North East Book Award 2010
Winner of the Portsmouth Book Award 2010
Winner of the Yorkshire Coast Book Award 2010

SOPHIE McKENZIE
SISTER, MISSING

SIMON AND SCHUSTER

First published in Great Britain in 2011 by Simon
and Schuster UK Ltd, a CBS company.

Copyright © 2011 Sophie McKenzie

Simon & Schuster UK Ltd
1st Floor, 222 Gray's Inn Road, London WC1X 8HB

A CIP catalogue record for this book is available from the British Library.

ISBN HB 978-0-85707-288-7
ISBN TPB 978-0-85707-341-9

1 3 5 7 9 10 8 6 4 2

Printed and bound by CPI Group (UK) Ltd, Croydon, CR0 4YY

www.simonandschuster.co.uk
www.sophiemckenziebooks.com

For my good friend, Philly

1

Sister

I woke up to sunshine pouring in through the bedroom window of the holiday cottage. It was going to be another hot day. I yawned and sat up in bed, careful not to disturb Madison. Her long dark hair was spread over the pillow. I brushed it gently back, revealing her sweet, heart-shaped face.

As I moved, Madison moaned in her sleep. Her lashes were long and dark against her soft cheek, but I could see the teardrops they still held. It had been like this every night since we'd arrived at the holiday cottage last week. A nightmare kept waking her – bringing her into my room, where I'd have to stroke her hair to get her back to sleep. Later, I'd wake to find her crying in her sleep . . . soft whimpers that broke my heart.

I bent down now and kissed her forehead, carefully drawing the quilt over her bare shoulder. I watched her for a moment as her breath grew less even and her eyes slowly opened.

'Hey, Lauren,' she mumbled. 'I was dreaming about Daddy again.'

'I know, babycakes,' I whispered. 'It's OK.'

Our father, Sam, had died suddenly nine months ago. Losing him was a big aching hole inside me, even though I didn't grow up with him. He was my birth dad but I had been kidnapped when I was tiny, and adopted, so I didn't know him until two years ago.

Sam had been really special and I missed him every day, but when I looked at my birth mum, Annie, or my sisters – Shelby and Madison – I could see that Sam dying so suddenly had been much worse for them . . . it had ripped their hearts out. Madison especially, being so young. She was only eight. My guts twisted thinking about how she must feel.

Now Madison nuzzled in close beside me. I stroked her hair and she yawned and stretched like a cat, arching her back and reaching her arms over her head. A moment later she was off the bed and scampering to the window. She turned to me with big brown eyes.

'Can we go to the beach today?'

I grinned at her. 'Sure – just as soon as you've had breakfast.'

'Yayy!!' Madison skipped round the room, her nightmares forgotten. She pulled on a pink tutu over her blue check pyjama bottoms. Her hair flew out behind her as she spun.

It suddenly struck me that I'd never understood that phrase: *a breath of fresh air*, before. But that was Madison – fresh air in a dull, flat world: the only person ever to raise a smile from Annie and the only person who always made me feel good about myself.

Madison stopped in mid-spin and stared at me. 'But no Shelby,' she said. 'Promise, Lauren. Shelby can't come too.'

I smiled. One of the many things that bound Madison and me together was a dislike of our middle sister. Shelby was *always* rude and aggressive. Only yesterday, she'd made Madison cry by sneering that she was too old to still be playing with dolls.

'Sure,' I said. 'If you get dressed really fast we'll be able to leave before she even wakes up.'

With a wide-eyed nod, Madison vanished from the room. I pulled on my clothes quickly, then checked myself in the mirror – the denim shorts, fitted T-shirt and sandals all looked OK. I took a straw bag from the wardrobe and fetched two towels and some sun cream from the bathroom. It had been amazingly hot for days, considering it was only April, and today looked like it was going to be no exception.

I tied my hair off my face and applied a little eyeliner and lip gloss. I slid the lip gloss into my bag along with my phone. Madison would enjoy playing with both of them while I hopefully tanned my legs. I already had a bikini top on under my T-shirt. Grabbing my sunglasses, I left the room.

Madison was downstairs, wolfing down a bowl of cereal.

'Well OK, you and Lauren can go, but only if you stay close together,' Annie said, twisting her hands anxiously over each other. She was wearing her dressing gown and yesterday's make-up.

'We'll be fine,' I said firmly. 'I'll look after Mo and —'

'But who'll look after *you*?' Annie interrupted. She picked up her coffee cup and sipped at it distractedly.

For goodness' sake. I gripped the sides of the table. I *wanted* to be sympathetic. I knew how hard losing Sam had hit her. It was hard for all of us. But why did she have to act like I was about to be kidnapped again every time I took two steps away from her? I was sixteen, and taking my GCSEs in a couple of months.

Swallowing down my irritation, I forced a smile on my face. 'We'll be fine,' I repeated.

'Don't you want to wait for Shelby to get up?' Annie asked.

'No, Mom,' Madison said firmly. 'We want to go *now*.' She stood up from the table and looped her little blue bag over her shoulder. I caught her eye, knowing what was inside the bag.

'OK, but . . . but are you sure you wouldn't rather go for a drive and a picnic?' Annie said.

Madison and I exchanged an alarmed glance. Annie's idea of a picnic consisted of a short journey during which she complained constantly about the narrow country lanes and having to drive on the 'wrong' side of the road, followed by a random meal based on whatever she'd found in the fridge. Over the past few days we'd sat on quite a few beaches, trying – and failing – to find one of the caves which Annie said the area was full of, and eating bizarre stuff like boiled egg and dried apricot salad . . . or, on one occasion, a packet of seeds that turned out to be bird food.

'Er . . . no thanks,' I said.

'OK, well, take this.' Annie shoved a couple of twenty-pound notes into my hand. 'Promise you'll be back by midday, OK?'

I rolled my eyes. 'All right.'

Madison raced across the room and put her bowl in the

sink. She was dressed in denim shorts and a T-shirt that was a similar blue to mine.

As both of us have long dark hair and the same easy-tan skin, our eyes (mine blue, Mo's dark brown) marked the only real colouring difference between us.

'Hey, we're twins, Mo,' I said.

'I know.' She beamed at me. 'I'm ready.'

'Take a jacket, both of you,' Annie said, bustling out to the coat stand in the hall.

'No need, it's already boiling out there.' I held out my hand and felt Madison's warm, small fingers curl round mine. 'Bye, Annie.'

'Bye, Mom,' called Madison. Giggling, she let me drag her out of the kitchen door and round the side of the house.

As she skipped down the pavement, still holding my hand, I could hear Annie's plaintive voice behind us. 'Be careful . . .' Irritation coiled round me like a snake.

We walked on. The sun beat down on my face, warming me through. The closer we got to the beach the happier I felt, the cloying weight of Annie's worry lifting as we left her behind.

It didn't occur to me for a second that she was right to worry . . . that there was anything *to* worry about.

And yet, two hours later, my whole world would be turned upside down. And, though I didn't know it at the time, it would all be my fault.

2

Missing

By 10 am the beach was starting to fill up with excited sunbathers. I guess it was the Easter Monday bank holiday and the unusually hot weather that was bringing people out, but to be honest I'd liked it better last week when the sky had been overcast and the seaside more deserted.

Madison didn't seem to mind. We stopped to watch the carousel on the promenade blaring out 'The Teddy Bear's Picnic', then found a spot on the sand and laid out our towels.

We'd done each other's hair – in tiny braids – and Madison was now curled up on her towel, picking at the edge of her little blue bag. She looked up at me, her huge chocolate-brown eyes betraying both eagerness and embarrassment.

'Go on,' I said with a smile. 'Get them out.'

Madison grinned back and gently retrieved the three pocket dolls I knew she kept inside the bag. As she started playing some imaginary game with them, whispering under her breath, I lay back and closed my eyes.

Before Sam died, Madison had more or less lost interest in her dolls, but afterwards she went right back to playing with them every day. At first Annie got all neurotic about it, worrying that Mo was 'acting out repressed grief' or some other fancy thing you needed a psychology degree to understand. After a bit she settled down about it, hoping that if she didn't make a fuss Mo would just gradually stop. Shelby, on the other hand, was vicious about it from day one. She teased Madison for being a baby every time she caught sight of a doll.

Neither of them understood. Madison just needed someone to love – someone who wasn't going to die on her.

Anyway, nine months on from Sam's death, Madison still played with her dolls – but only alone, or with me.

'How's Tilda today?' I said, pointing to a particularly cute doll with red hair and freckles.

'She got mad at Tammy,' Madison said, shaking her head sorrowfully. 'Tilda was mean.' She went on to explain the ins and outs of the imaginary argument.

I got lost after a few minutes, but I nodded and smiled anyway. After she'd finished her explanation, I checked she had enough sun lotion on her bare legs, then picked up my phone and logged onto Facebook. It was early still, but most of my friends – and my boyfriend Jam – were in London over Easter and I knew loads of them had met up yesterday evening.

If we hadn't hired this holiday home I could have gone out with them. But since Sam died from some undiagnosed heart condition, Annie had only visited the UK twice and both times she'd refused to set foot in their London flat, which was why we'd ended up here, in Norbourne on the south coast of England, this Easter.

I'd considered protesting about spending two weeks away from all my friends, but Annie just burst into tears every time I talked about London, while Mum and Dad thought me being away from the distractions of home for two weeks was a brilliant idea.

Just as I thought of her, Mum texted me. I hesitated to open the message. Things weren't that great between me and Mum just then. You see, though Annie is my biological mother, Mum and Dad are the ones who've brought me up. I live with them during term time, then visit my US family in the holidays. Last week Annie and my sisters had come over from the States to spend the holidays with me, while Mum, Dad and my little brother Rory went to Disney World for a fortnight.

With a sigh, I opened Mum's text.

How is the revision going? Remember three hours every morning. Then you will have the rest of the day to play! Love Mum x

Growling with irritation, I closed the text without replying.

Surely it wasn't supposed to be like this? I'd always tried to be grateful for having two mothers who cared about me, but right now it felt like I had two jailers. On the one hand there was anxious, needy Annie who wanted to lock me away from the world to keep me safe and on the other there was Mum – nagging away like she was head of the Revision Police.

'Hey, Lauren, look at Tammy,' Madison said.

I glanced over. Tammy, I knew, was Madison's favourite pocket doll – a chubby, round-faced miniature version of

Madison herself, with long dark hair and huge brown eyes framed with long, lush lashes.

'I'm putting her hair in braids too,' Madison said.

'Cool.' I examined the two neat plaits that Madison had carefully tied with threads from her towel. 'Nice job.'

Madison beamed and bent over the doll again.

I turned back to my phone and checked to see who was online. A couple of friends were chatting, but not Jam. Maybe it was just as well. We'd drifted apart a bit recently. He said he was trying to give me space after Sam's death and while we were both studying for our GCSEs, but I couldn't help wondering if he was losing interest. I know I could have asked, but I didn't want to make myself look vulnerable. So I'd been holding back too, waiting to see what he did . . . how he acted.

Across the beach a group of teenagers were gathering outside the Boondog Shack café. I hadn't been inside yet, but it looked fun, the sort of place Jam and I would go. My fingers drifted to the wooden oval he'd given me two years ago. I still wore it round my neck most of the time. I wasn't sure Jam even noticed.

Beside me, Madison sat up. 'Can I get an ice cream?'

'Sure.' I fished in my shorts pocket for the money Annie had given me. 'There's a stall just over there. We can leave the towels.'

Madison frowned as she followed my pointing finger. 'Please can I go by myself?' she said. 'It's only over there.'

I hesitated. If I'm honest, part of me worried about Madison almost as much as Annie did. You don't survive two kidnappings and a murder attempt without becoming aware of how ugly the world can be.

'*Please*,' Madison persisted. 'Mommy never lets me do anything and I'm almost nine.'

'You're not nine until November,' I said.

But I knew I was going to let her go. After all, Annie was ridiculously overprotective which wasn't good for Madison. And I could actually see the ice cream stall from our spot on the beach. Nothing could happen to her. Nothing *would*. It was a sunny morning and most of the people about were families with small children, laughing and splashing in the sea or building sandcastles. Plus, Mo had her own phone, tucked safely at the bottom of her bag.

'Here.' I handed her one of Annie's twenty-pound notes. 'Get me whatever you're having and make sure he gives you the right change, OK?'

'Sure. I'll get Twisters.' Madison beamed at me. She slid her doll, Tammy, into her pocket and trotted off across the sand. I stood up, watching her as she reached the promenade and crossed to the stall. I could see the man behind it leaning forward, clearly trying to hear her order, and Madison shaking her head impatiently, hands on hips.

As I watched, the man handed her the ice lollies and Madison reached up to give him the money.

'Hey there.' A boy's voice beside me made me jump. 'Have you seen Cassie?'

I looked around. The guy was in his late teens, wearing long shorts and a faded T-shirt with *Boondog Shack* written on the front. He was totally gorgeous: tanned, blond and square-jawed like a model, and, for a second, I was so shocked, both by his appearance and by the fact that he was standing so close to me, that my mouth actually fell open. I took a step backwards, almost stumbling on the sand. The boy caught my arm and smiled as he steadied me.

'Have you seen Cassie?' he repeated.

'I don't know anyone called Cassie,' I said.

'Oh, OK.' He smiled again. 'Sorry to bother you.' He sauntered off.

I blinked, then remembered Madison and turned back to the ice cream stall. I couldn't see her. She should have been on her way back across the beach towards me by now. Maybe she'd got confused and wandered off in the wrong direction. I scanned the horizon. The beach was fairly crowded, but there was still plenty of space between the groupings on the sand and I had a clear view for at least two hundred metres in both directions.

'Mo!' I called.

Several nearby families looked around. Ignoring them, I yelled again. 'MO!' *Where was she?* It wasn't like her to muck about.

My shout echoed away into silence. My guts squeezed into a knot. *Don't panic*, I said to myself. *It's only been a few seconds. She's got to be here somewhere.*

Still scanning the beach, I grabbed my phone and called her number. But Madison's mobile was switched off. I groaned out loud. Why hadn't I checked it was on when she'd walked away? I picked up my straw bag and headed towards the stall. I kept glancing over my shoulder, but there was nothing behind me except our towels on the ground. If Madison came back she'd see them and wait for me. My eyes strained across the sand and along the promenade, skipping over each figure, looking for those chestnut braids. She couldn't have just vanished.

I reached the ice cream stall. The vendor was chatting to two elderly ladies as he held a cone under his ice cream machine.

'Excuse me,' I interrupted. 'The little girl you served just now, did you see where she went?'

The man frowned. I could feel the elderly ladies looking at me.

'Little girl?' the man said slowly.

'Yes,' I said. 'She's eight and a half with brown eyes and long brown hair in plaits. She . . . she ordered two Twisters and gave you a twenty-pound note like about two minutes ago. Less.'

The man nodded. 'I remember.'

I glanced round again. A soft breeze was playing across the beach. The sky was a clear blue. Children's laughter filled the air. Madison must be here somewhere, maybe just around the corner.

'So did you see where she went?' I turned back to the man.
He shrugged.

One of the two elderly women he was serving cleared her throat. 'Perhaps she's in the ladies,' she said, pointing round the side of the stall.

12

Nodding, I rushed past them. The ladies' loo was clearly marked just along the promenade wall. I darted inside, but all the cubicles were empty, their doors hanging open. A woman was putting on lipstick at the mirror.

'Did a little girl just come in here?' I asked.

The woman shook her head. I rushed outside and glanced back across the beach. Our towels were still lying where I'd left them. No sign of Madison.

Fighting back my rising panic, I stopped and took a deep breath. *Think. Where could she have gone?* I turned right around, looking in every direction, trying to spot the familiar silhouette of my little sister. But there was no sign of her.

Heart pounding, I grabbed the arm of a mother walking by, her baby in a sling.

'My sister's missing,' I said. 'She's eight and a half.'

'Oh.' The woman's eyes widened. She raised her hand protectively over her baby's head, as if to shield her from the news. 'I'm . . . er . . . that's terrible. What happened?'

'She went to buy an ice cream and she hasn't come back.' As I spoke, my eyes scanned the beach again, desperately hoping I'd catch a glimpse of Madison in her denim shorts and blue T-shirt.

'When?' the woman asked.

'Not long. A few minutes ago,' I said.

The woman's face relaxed. 'She's probably just gone in the wrong direction. Got lost, not paying attention to where she was—'

'No.' I shook my head. 'Madison isn't like that.'

13

The woman with the baby took a step away from me. Her expression registered sympathy but distance. She didn't want to get involved. 'I'm sure your sister will turn up,' she said. 'Have you tried the ladies?'

'Yes.' The word snapped out of me. I spun around, searching the beach again. 'D'you know if there's a lifeguard here?'

The woman shook her head. 'Not on this stretch, sorry.' She walked off. I looked along the path after her and my breath caught in my throat.

Two Twisters, still in their wrappers, were lying on the tarmac, melting. Were those the ice lollies Madison had just bought?

I took a step towards them. I gasped. Just beyond the Twisters lay Madison's pocket doll, Tammy. She was face down on the ground, her shoes missing and one of her plaits untwisting in the sunshine.

And that's when I knew.

Madison hadn't wandered off, or gone in the wrong direction by mistake. Something really, really bad had happened.

I picked up the doll and shoved it in my straw bag. The world spun inside my head. I had to act. I had to do something . . .

I strode off across the sand. It was warm and soft, hard to walk in. Earlier I'd enjoyed the way the grains trickled up between my toes, but now it was awful not being able to move faster.

'Mo!' I yelled as I hurried along. 'Madison!'

14

Maybe she just dropped the doll. Maybe she got lost. I muttered under my breath, trying – and failing – to reassure myself. *Please, Mo.*

Surely she would appear any second – plaits streaming out behind her as she raced towards me.

But she didn't.

I headed for our two towels, still lined up on the sand, just a few metres from the sea. The whole area was busier than it had been even just a few minutes ago and I knew I was never going to spot Madison in the crowds. Hoping against hope, I called her again, but her mobile was still switched off. I held my own phone in my hand – in case she called me – as I stopped to work through my options.

I knew I had to tell Annie. I didn't want to, but short of contacting the police I couldn't see what else to do. I glanced around, forcing myself to focus on every detail.

Please be here, Mo. Please.

Up on the promenade a group of teenagers were chatting outside the Boondog Shack. The boy who'd spoken to me earlier was with them. He'd obviously found the girl *he'd* been looking for.

Families were still swarming onto the beach. Shrieks and yells filled the air. There were plenty of little kids . . . toddlers in sunhats waving toy plastic spades, a pair of skinny redheads in matching Bermuda shorts . . . an overweight girl about Madison's age wearing a bright pink dress.

I stood, trying to see everything all at once. It was no good. Panic rose inside me, whipping up through my body like a tornado.

And then my phone beeped. A text from Madison's phone. Relief surged through me. With trembling hands, I opened the text.

Stop looking on the beach. Your sister isn't there. Do NOT contact the police or I will kill her. Go home and wait.

3

The Wait

I stared at the words, the sun beating down on the back of my head. Madison had been taken. She was missing, just as I had once been. My legs gave way underneath me and I sank to the sand. I read the text again and again. Trying to make the words sink in.

I looked up. The world on the beach was carrying on as normal. But everything had changed. I got to my feet and walked, blindly, across the sand. My heart was beating so fast and so loudly I could barely hear myself think.

Who could have taken her? Where was she?

I looked around. The car park was out of sight behind the row of beach huts. If Madison was no longer on the beach maybe she was there. I broke into a run. Then stopped. If Madison had been bundled into a car she would be well away from the car park by now. I felt numb as I reached the promenade and stopped to slip on my sandals. I'd left the towels, I realised, and turned to go back for them. Then I stopped. What did it matter if I lost a couple of beach towels? Madison had been in my care and I'd allowed someone to take her.

I looked at the text message again.

Do NOT contact the police.

17

I needed to tell Annie.

My stomach twisted into a hard ball of knots as I ran hard up the road, back to the holiday home. Annie was hunched over the kitchen sink, her back towards the door. She was dressed now and humming to herself as I walked in.

I stood in the doorway. How on earth could I even begin to explain to her what had happened?

'Is that you, Madison sweetie? Lauren?'

I said nothing. My legs felt like lead.

Annie turned round. She blinked as she took in the fact that I was alone. 'Where's Madison?'

I couldn't find the words to say it, so I just held out my phone. Annie stared at my face and her mouth fell open. In a second she was across the room. She grabbed my mobile and read the text. Her lips moved as she went over the words. Like me, she read it three times before she looked up. Her face was ghost-white, her eyes filled with horror.

'No,' she wailed. 'No, not again!' She threw the phone onto the kitchen table where, just a few hours before, Madison had sat grinning at me over her cereal bowl.

I picked up my phone and closed the text.

'What are we going to do?' I said.

My voice shook as I spoke and I realised how much I'd been hoping Annie would somehow *know* what to do.

But Annie collapsed into a chair and started rocking backwards and forwards, moaning softly to herself. Like me, her eyes were tearless. This was too big, too terrifying for tears.

18

I sat down opposite her, feeling numb. I had a sudden urge to call Jam – or Mum – but that would have involved movement and action. And I didn't feel capable of either.

I tried to concentrate. We had two options. Call the police – and risk Mo's life. Or wait for a phone call, as the kidnappers had ordered.

Footsteps sounded upstairs, padding across the landing.

'That'll be Shelby,' Annie said in a dull, flat voice. 'Will you tell her what's going on?'

I stood up, resentment swirling through my numb fear for Madison. Shelby was likely to have hysterics when she heard Madison was missing – and Annie knew it. Why did I have to be the one to deal with her?

'Please, Lauren.' Her voice cracked. 'I can't handle this.'

My shaking legs somehow carried me into the hallway of the holiday house. Shelby was padding down the stairs. She was dressed in sweatpants and a shapeless camisole, her dyed hair all tousled and her eyes sleepy. It was just past 11.30 am which, for Shelby, was an early start to the day. Annie always gave her a hard time for getting up late. Personally I was delighted at any opportunity not to have to deal with her. Shelby was only a year younger than me, but we had never got on. I'd tried to be friendly when we'd first met, but Shelby had thrown all my attempts to be nice back in my face. She reached the bottom of the stairs and scowled at me.

'What?' she said.

Behind me I could hear Annie tapping into her phone.

'Someone's taken Madison from the beach,' I said. 'They've sent a text saying not to contact the police. They'll call us later.'

Shelby's mouth dropped open, much as Annie's had done earlier. They looked a lot alike, actually, though Shelby had longer hair and spots.

'No way,' she said, running her hand over her forehead. 'You're yanking my chain.'

'I wouldn't joke about this,' I snapped, turning and stalking back into the kitchen.

Shelby followed me in. Annie was bent over her phone, talking in a low voice, but Shelby paid no attention.

'What's going on, Mom?' she said.

Annie put down her phone with a sigh and repeated what I'd already said.

Shelby's mouth trembled as the reality of the news hit home. 'No!' she shrieked. 'No *way*.'

Annie opened her arms. 'I know, sweetie, come—'

'This is your fault.' Shelby turned on me, her finger jabbing at my face.

'*What?*' I stared at her.

'It's a copycat of *your* kidnapping. Off a freakin' beach and everything,' Shelby yelled.

My mouth fell open. I hadn't made the connection myself but it was true. Fourteen years ago *I* had gone missing on a beach not that different from the one Madison and I had been on earlier. I'd been playing hide-and-seek with Annie and I'd been taken by Sonia Holtwood. She kept me for a while, then sold me through an agency to my adoptive parents, pretending to be a poverty-stricken single mother.

Holtwood had tried to kill me and Madison two years ago, when I found out what she'd done and tracked Annie and Sam down. She was in jail now, serving a long term for kidnap and attempted murder.

'Shelby, don't be silly . . .' Annie started.

'Have you called the police?' Shelby demanded, wild-eyed.

'We told you, the text said not to,' I said sharply.

'And we're just going to do what we're told?' Shelby's voice rose in another shriek.

'Calm down,' I said.

'Shut up!' she shouted.

'Please, girls,' Annie said, sobbing.

Shelby stormed off and the kitchen fell silent as her footsteps faded up the stairs.

Annie sighed and put her head in her hands. 'I've called Rick,' she said. 'He'll be here soon.'

'Right.' Rick was Annie's new boyfriend – a British guy she'd met on her last visit to see me. They'd become close in the past few months. I knew Rick had flown over from London to visit her in the States at least twice since then.

I'd only met him a few times myself. He'd seemed nice – a charming ex-security guard in his late thirties with beefy arms, a receding hairline and a warm smile. I wasn't quite sure what he saw in Annie, but he acted as a calming presence around her which helped make her easier to deal with.

Madison seemed to like him too. At the thought of her,

panic surged through me, exploding my previous numbness with the force of a bomb. This was stupid, us just waiting for a call. Madison had disappeared at about five past eleven and it was now almost midday. Images of her bundled up in the back of someone's car being driven away from the beach, terrified, filled my head. She could be miles away by now. She could be hurt. And why had she been taken? What would anyone want with her? Surely a psycho wouldn't send a text saying she'd been kidnapped if he was planning on murdering her.

Would he?

'Maybe Shelby's right,' I said, pacing across the room. 'Maybe we *should* call the police.'

'No.' Annie looked up. 'We can't take the risk. Not until we know what they want . . . what they're threatening to do to Madison.'

She was right. Shuddering, I sat down beside her at the kitchen table. I don't know how long we sat there – it felt like ages.

'Oh God, oh God,' Annie kept muttering.

I bit my lip. I couldn't *bear* just sitting here. We had to do something.

My phone rang. Madison's number again.

Annie stared at me as I picked up the mobile.

'Hello?' I said.

'Lauren?' The voice was female but disguised – filtered through some kind of machine that made it sound robot-like. 'Are you at home, like I asked?'

'Yes,' I said. 'Where's Madison? Is she all right?'

22

Annie was on her feet beside me now, twisting her hands anxiously over each other.

The voice continued: 'Madison is safe and well. If you do what I say she'll be returned home shortly.' The voice paused. 'So how are *you* doing, Lauren?'

'I want to speak to Madison. Hear for myself that she's all right.'

'Not yet.' The voice grew tense. 'You always were a little princess, weren't you? Looking down your nose at everyone else.'

I froze. Did this woman *know* me?

'Who are you?' I asked.

The woman laughed. It sounded weird through the robot-like filler. 'Don't you remember me, Lauren?'

My mind flashed back to Shelby's words: *This is your fault . . . it's a copycat of your kidnapping . . .*

The connections snapped together in my mind.

Could Madison's kidnapper be the same person who had abducted me all those years ago?

4

An Old Connection

As soon as I'd thought this, I rejected the idea. It wasn't possible. The woman who'd kidnapped me – Sonia Holtwood – was in jail.

'What do you want?' I stammered.

The woman laughed again. 'Listen and I'll explain.' She told me to go to Sandcove Chine – one of the steep, wooded ravines near the coast – and wait by the Japanese pond.

'Be there in half an hour. I'll give you the proof you want that Madison is alive and instructions about what to do next. And make sure you're alone,' she said. 'Just you, Lauren. Just you.'

Before I could reply, she rang off. Annie, who'd been standing right next to me throughout the phone call, drew her breath in sharply.

'What did they say, Lauren?'

I told her. As I spoke, my mind kept going over how the woman had asked if I remembered her. It just didn't make sense – unless she *was* Sonia Holtwood.

'Sandcove Chine is just a few minutes' walk from here.' Annie frowned. 'I don't understand. Why didn't the woman say what she wants on the phone? Why make you go somewhere else to get this "proof"?'

'Maybe she's worried we'll record the call or something.' I shrugged. 'Maybe she's going to follow me . . . make sure we haven't contacted the police.' A shiver ran down my spine at the prospect.

'OK.' Annie frowned. 'But why does she only want to deal with you?'

I took a deep breath. I had to tell Annie what I suspected, even though it was going to sound ridiculous. 'I think she knows me,' I said. 'I know it's crazy, but I think she might be Sonia Holtwood.'

Annie's face paled.

'But Sonia Holtwood's in prison,' Shelby said from the doorway. She must have walked over while I was on the phone. I hadn't noticed her standing there.

'No, she's not.' Annie's voice trembled as she spoke.

'What d'you mean?' I said.

'Mom?' Shelby twisted her hair round her fingers.

'Sonia Holtwood was released from jail two months ago,' Annie said. 'There was an appeal . . . a technicality . . . They overturned her conviction. Everyone knows she's guilty, but she never admitted it and now she's free.'

I gasped. 'Why didn't you tell me?'

'And me?' Shelby added.

'I spoke to your mother and father about it, Lauren. I . . . I actually wanted to say something, but they didn't want to upset you,' Annie said. 'We were all going through so much, what with losing Sam and . . .'

'My exams . . .' I said, imagining Mum's concern.

Fury rose in me – this was *so* typical of Mum and Dad, always assuming they knew what was best for me. How dare they keep such massive news from me. Sonia Holtwood had targeted me directly before. I had a right to know if she was free. And now she had Madison.

Before I could say anything, my phone rang again.

'Is that her?' Shelby asked.

I glanced down. *Jam calling.*

'No,' I said, relief swamping my anger.

'Hi,' I said into the phone. I walked past both Annie and Shelby towards the stairs.

'Hey, Lazerbrain.' Jam's voice – so familiar and so warm – brought a lump to my throat. 'How's it going at the seaside?'

'Oh, Jam.' I was close to tears as I told him everything that had happened.

He listened carefully – Jam's always been a good listener.

'Man, that's terrible—' Just as Jam started to speak, the call dropped.

I checked my signal. It was fine. I waited a second. Surely Jam would call back. Nothing happened. I tried ringing him, but the call went to voice mail.

That was strange. Feeling doubly anxious now, I walked back into the kitchen only to discover Shelby and Annie both crying.

'I hate Rick,' Shelby wept. 'He's always interfering in our business and turning up when we don't want him around.'

'But I *do* want him around,' Annie wailed. 'He's a good friend.'

26

'To *you*.' Shelby's voice rose to a shriek. 'What about *me*? What about what *I* want?'

'This situation isn't about you, Shelby,' I snapped. Honestly, what a selfish cow. 'It's about Madison and trying to get her back.'

'Shut UP!' Shelby yelled and stormed out of the room.

We could hear her bawling all the way up the stairs, then the slam of her bedroom door.

Annie shook her head and collapsed into a kitchen chair. I checked the time. As Annie had said, it would only take a few minutes to walk to Sandcove Chine. There were still twenty minutes until I had to be there, but at least once I set off I'd be doing something. I guess I should have been scared at the thought of coming up against Sonia Holtwood but, right then, all I could think about was saving Mo.

'I'm going,' I said.

'No.' Annie looked up at me, panic-stricken. 'It's too early. Rick will be here any minute. At least wait until he gets here.'

'OK.' I didn't really want to wait, but Annie looked so desperate I felt I had to. My head was swirling with a million emotions, but I held all of them in. What I'd said to Shelby about focusing on Madison applied just as much to me. I couldn't afford to break down. I was the strongest person here, and I had to *stay* strong for my little sister.

Rick arrived a few minutes later. Annie, who'd been hovering by the door, flung herself into his arms.

'Don't worry, pet,' he said, stroking her hair. 'I'm here now. We'll get Madison back. I was in security for fifteen years, remember?'

'But it's only Lauren they want to deal with,' Annie explained shakily.

'So you said.' Rick sat her down at the kitchen table. He looked concerned. 'What's that about, then?'

'I think the kidnapper might be the woman who tried to kill me two years ago,' I said. 'Sonia Holtwood.'

'Who?' Rick asked.

Annie explained the history and Rick's expression of concern deepened. As Annie spoke, I found myself feeling annoyed with her again. She should have told me months ago about Sonia Holtwood being free. On the other hand, I couldn't really blame Annie. She was just doing what Mum and Dad told her. When were they going to realise they didn't have to treat me like a little kid any more?

'What I don't understand is *why* Sonia Holtwood would have taken the little one,' Rick said, looking from me to Annie. 'What's the point?'

Annie shook her head despairingly.

'I think it's got something to do with getting back at me, but . . . but I don't know what exactly,' I said.

Rick nodded slowly. 'Well, one thing's for sure,' he said. 'I'm not letting you go to Sandcove Chine alone. I'll hang back so I can't be seen, but I'm definitely going to be right there behind you.'

'Oh, Rick, thank you,' Annie gasped.

He looked at me. 'Is that OK with you, Lauren?'

'Hey, excuse me, but are you *seriously* not calling the police?' Shelby's voice echoed across the hallway.

We turned round. She was standing at the bottom of the stairs, her fists clenched and resting on her hips.

'Oh, sweetie, you don't understand . . .' Annie began.

'Don't patronise me,' Shelby snapped. 'Why aren't we calling the cops, Mom?'

'Because the kidnapper said she'd kill Madison if we did that,' I said, trying to keep my temper. 'And if she really *is* Sonia Holtwood then she definitely isn't bluffing. She's capable of murder.'

Shelby turned to Annie. 'Mom, are you seriously going to listen to *her* instead of me?'

I dug my fingers into my palms, desperately trying not to lose control.

'This isn't a popularity contest, Shelby,' I insisted. 'The point is that Holtwood is a killer.'

Annie turned helplessly to Rick. 'What do *you* think?'

'Why are you asking him?' Shelby snapped.

We all looked at Rick. A moment passed, then he cleared his throat.

'From what I understand of the situation – and when I worked in security I heard about quite a few kidnap cases –' he said slowly, 'it makes sense for Lauren to at least go to Sandcove Chine. It's a public place and this is the middle of the day. I'm sure the kidnappers only want to draw her outside to make sure she's not being trailed by the police. She can get proof Madison's alive and find out what the deal is . . . I'll be right there with her, so . . .'

Shelby swore and stomped upstairs again.

Annie looked distraught but, to be honest, I was glad Shelby had gone. She was a nightmare and her presence only ever made things worse.

Even at 1.15 pm, the ravine at Sandcove Chine was cool and shady. The heat of the day was still fierce, but out of the sun there was a chilly breeze. As I walked, shivering, I hugged my jacket round my chest. Ahead of me, the Japanese pond glinted in the sunlight. A few elderly couples were strolling past. Others sat on the benches opposite the water.

Mum had sent me another text just a couple of minutes before, asking how my revision had gone today. Up to that point I'd been seriously considering calling her at Disney World and telling her everything that had happened. But the text made me think twice. Mum would absolutely forbid me to make any contact with Madison's kidnappers. And I was pretty certain she'd be on Shelby's side over calling the police too. Anyway, I was still furious with her for not telling me Sonia Holtwood was out of prison.

I reached the pond. Feeling nervous, I glanced up the ravine to where I knew Rick was watching. We'd swapped numbers earlier, which meant I could call him if I saw anything weird. As my fingers hovered over his number, just in case, he sent a text himself.

I can see you, kid. Any trouble I'll be with you in less than a minute.

Slightly reassured, I leaned against the tree at my back. The ground all around was dry and hard. It hadn't rained for days My phone buzzed again. This time the text was from a with-held number. I opened it quickly.

Path left of pond. Thirty metres. Broken bench. Look underneath.

It was the kidnapper. I glanced ahead, into the shadowy path that led away from the pond. The first bench was missing the two slats at the back. I jogged over. There was no sign of anyone – though I knew Rick was still watching over me up the ravine – and no sound other than the wind in the trees and the distant sound of the sea sucking at the shore.

My fingers trembled as I felt along the rough wooden under-side of the bench. A padded envelope was taped to the slats. I ripped it off and tore it open. Inside was Madison's phone. As I picked it up, it beeped with a video message.

I watched, my heart thumping, as Madison's face filled the screen.

'Lauren?' she said. Her lips wobbled and tears welled in her big brown eyes. 'This message is for you.'

A lump rose in my throat. I couldn't bear to see her so frightened and upset.

Madison turned her head, clearly looking towards some-one in the corner of the room, off camera. A second later she picked up a piece of paper from her lap, tucked her hair behind her ear and gave a sniff. In a shaky voice she read out loud:

'The woman who has me knows us because of you, Lauren. She wants the money from Daddy's will.'

I blinked. Sam's money? Was that what this was all about?

'You have to have the two million pounds life in . . . insur-ance . . .' My heart seemed to tear a little as Madison stumbled over the word and looked anxiously into the corner of the room again. *'. . . ready in cash by tomorrow morning . . .'*

My grip tightened on the phone. I knew very little about Sam's life insurance . . . only that he'd arranged that, if he died, Annie would be entitled to a huge lump sum, and that she had finally received the money the week before she arrived in Britain.

On the screen, tears were now streaming down Madison's face. 'I don't know where I am, Lauren, if you're there, but I'm really scared and this woman is mean. I haven't seen her face, but she's American.'

At that point the screen fizzled into silence. I stared at it, panic clutching at my throat. The kidnapper *must be* Sonia Holtwood. She had to be. All that stuff about her knowing us because of me. Plus, she was clearly from the States. And why else would she be hiding her face if she wasn't scared Madison would recognise her?

A twig cracked behind me. I jumped. Spun round.

'Who's there?' I said. 'Rick?'

'No.' And then the last person I expected to see stepped out of the shadows.

5

The Money

'Jam?' I stared at him, taking in his broad shoulders and handsome, square-jawed face. All so familiar and yet still so gorgeous to me.

Since we started going out two years ago, Jam had grown several centimetres and was now a head taller than me, but the warmth in his hazel eyes was just the same.

He held out his arms and I stumbled into them, feeling a weight lift from my back. In spite of the terrible situation poor Madison was in – and my own feelings of guilt – there was something about Jam's presence that had always made me feel better. I took a deep breath, smelling his familiar scent: part soap, part unique Jam-ness.

'I thought you were still in London,' I said, astonished.

'Nah, I was on my way when I called you. I was about to explain, but my battery died.' Jam slicked back his dark hair and hugged me hard. 'What on earth are you doing, Lazerbrain? I got to your holiday home and saw Annie . . . man, I couldn't believe she'd let you come here alone.'

'I'm not alone,' I said, looking up the ravine to where Rick was now running towards us. 'Annie's friend Rick is watching over me.'

'Yeah, Annie said.' Jam hesitated. 'Still, anything could have—'

'I'm fine,' I insisted. 'The kidnapper said it had to be just me . . . alone. Oh, Jam, I think it's Sonia Holtwood.'

Jam's eyes widened. But before he could say anything, Rick grabbed him by the shoulders and shoved him away from me.

'Who are you?' Rick demanded.

'He's my . . . my boyfriend,' I said, blushing at having to explain. Rick and Jam hadn't met before, of course. I mean, *I'd* only met Rick a few times. I quickly told both of them what the kidnapper had told me to do and the three of us walked back to the holiday home. We didn't say much. Rick called Annie as we strode along. I could hear her on the other end of the line, totally freaking out. She was waiting anxiously at the front door when we arrived, Shelby skulking like a shadow behind her.

It took about thirty minutes before Annie stopped crying long enough for the five of us to have a proper conversation. Annie herself did most of the talking or, rather, most of the hysterical wailing. She leaned against Rick as if he were all that was stopping her from falling to the floor and alternated between extreme anxiety over Madison and profound terror at having to deal with Sonia Holtwood.

Rick, Jam and I examined Madison's phone carefully, but it gave us no clues about anything. The video message showing Madison had obviously been filmed in an empty room. All we could see behind Mo's head was a plain painted wall. And the sender's name was, again, withheld.

34

Annie gasped when I told her how much money the kidnapper was after.

'The whole two million pounds from Sam's life insurance?' she said, her hands trembling. 'But that was our future. I was going to invest it. I was . . .'

'That's not all,' I said, explaining next how I was sure Holtwood was behind the whole thing.

'Oh my God,' she kept saying, over and over, her hands fluttering to her chest. 'Then it really is happening again. I can't believe it. Not Sonia Holtwood.'

'Never mind her now,' Rick said in a soothing voice. 'You need to focus on getting the money together. The sooner you do that, the sooner we'll get Madison back and this whole thing will be behind us.'

'That's right.' Annie gripped Rick's arm more tightly. 'I'll call my bank back home. The money went into my account last week so—'

'The kidnapper must know that,' I said. 'It's too big a coincidence otherwise.'

'But how could she?' Annie said shakily. 'How do they know the exact amount?'

'Maybe she was able to hack into the bank's account details,' Rick said.

'Or maybe she has someone on the inside at the bank, keeping her informed,' Jam suggested.

'Or maybe she just followed the story of Sam's death in the papers,' I offered. 'If she knew there was going to be an insurance payment, and she knew where you lived, it wouldn't be that hard to track you to the bank and get the details. She could have bribed someone to tell her.'

'Oh my goodness.' Another fat tear rolled down Annie's cheek. 'I can't bear this.'

I shivered. However Sonia Holtwood had done it, it was horrible to feel she'd been watching and waiting, following the progress of Sam's money into Annie's bank account.

'You'll have to get your bank to wire you the money here,' Rick said thoughtfully.

'Yes.' Annie nodded. 'I'm sure that'll work, even if I have to go to a local office here to sign for it.'

'Or we could call the police,' Shelby said angrily. 'See what they advise.'

'No.' Annie and I spoke at once.

'Shelby, don't you get it?' I said. 'I'm almost certain the kidnapper is Sonia Holtwood. She says she'll kill Madison if we contact the police. And she will. Come on, you *know* she's capable of . . .'

'Will you stay, Rick? Come with me if I have to go anywhere?' Annie pleaded. 'I can't do this alone.'

'Of course,' Rick said.

'No!' Shelby's lip trembled. 'Why do you have to do everything Lauren and Rick tell you, Mom?'

For goodness' sake.

'Maybe because Rick and I aren't stupid and hysterical,' I said.

Shelby threw down her coffee cup. 'You always think you're right, don't you, Lauren?'

36

'This isn't about me being right, this is about Mad—'

'Yeah, you're always sucking up to Madison too, thinking she's so cute still playing with her stupid dolls,' Shelby interrupted. 'The two of you always leave me out of everything.'

'What?' I couldn't believe what Shelby was saying. *She* was the one who pushed *us* away.

'I hate you,' Shelby yelled. 'It's your fault no-one listens to me.' And with that, she stormed out of the room.

Annie looked at me reproachfully. 'Please don't wind her up, Lauren.'

'Right,' I said, feeling aggrieved. I mean, what had I ever done to Shelby that justified her being so rude?

The wait until we had the money in our hands was hell. Annie spent an agonising hour on the phone to her bank in the States, then the rest of the afternoon with Rick, sorting out the international wire transfer at an office in Southampton, just along the coast. She returned exhausted, having had to fill out multiple forms, repeat her password endlessly and sign in triplicate for the cash.

'We can pick up the money in the morning,' she said, white-faced, then disappeared upstairs to lie down. Rick and Shelby followed her, while Jam went out to buy us all fish and chips.

I was left alone downstairs. Silent minutes ticked past. I paced up and down the kitchen. There was nothing I could do until tomorrow morning which seemed like a million years away.

37

Hold on, Mo, I repeated in my head like a prayer. *Hold on, we're going to get you back.*

I just hoped she wasn't hurt. Still, why would Sonia Holtwood – and I was more and more certain that she was the kidnapper – harm Madison? She must know that we would only hand over the money if Madison was OK.

Shouts issued from upstairs. I went into the hall. Shelby was yelling again about how everyone was ignoring her. A second later she stormed down the stairs, past me and out into the garden, slamming the kitchen door behind her.

Selfish cow. How could she go on and on about not being listened to, as if this whole situation was about her? Didn't she realise how terrified Madison must be, spending the night alone with Sonia Holtwood?

Nothing else mattered to me except getting Madison back. And though there was no reason why Sonia Holtwood wouldn't let her go once she had her two million, anxiety gnawed through me like a rat on a rope.

I could hear Annie sobbing in her bedroom. Should I go up and try and comfort her? No, Rick was there. I could hear his voice now, soft and low, attempting to calm her down.

I walked back into the kitchen and sat down at the table. My heart literally hurt inside my chest. How could my little sister be gone? I couldn't bear it.

My phone rang. It was Mum . . . calling from Disney World. I let it go to voice mail. My head was too full of worry about Madison to explain everything again – *and* deal with Mum's reaction.

38

'Missed your phone call?' Shelby's thin, accusing voice came from the garden doorway.

I looked up. Her eyes were red from crying, but the fierce look of disdain on her face made it impossible to feel sorry for her.

I pocketed my phone.

'Don't let me stop you calling him back.' Shelby's tone was scathing. 'We all know how you can't get through a whole hour without speaking to your boyfriend.'

'It wasn't Jam actually,' I said.

'No?' Shelby sniffed. 'I noticed he couldn't wait to get away from you earlier.'

I stared at my sister. Was that true? Surely Jam had gone out to get fish and chips because he was a nice person who could see Annie was in no state to think about cooking any dinner – not to get away from me. I mean, like I said, he'd been a bit distant recently, but he still wanted to be with me. Coming here today proved it, didn't it?

Either way, Shelby was just being mean.

'What's your problem, Shelby?' I snapped. 'Your *real* problem, I mean, apart from what you *should* be worrying about which is Madison and what you obviously *are* worrying about which is the state of my love life.'

She hesitated. Then to my surprise she sank down in the nearest chair and twisted her hands together, exactly as I'd seen Annie do.

'We should be calling the police,' she said. 'I know Mom and Rick are totally against it, but the police would know what to do. They're in the best position to get Madison back.'

Now Shelby's haughty mask had slipped, I could see how scared she was. For the first time I seriously wondered if she had a point. The police were experts at dealing with kidnapping and ransom demands, which I certainly wasn't, while Annie was an emotional wreck. As for Rick, well, his work as a security guard, or whatever he'd done, didn't exactly make him James Bond.

Perhaps the police *were* in the best position to help Madison.

I looked up at Shelby, ready to discuss it at least. Her dyed hair was a mess, blonde strands falling over her face and at least five centimetres of root showing. Somehow it made her look more vulnerable. I felt pity for her. After all, Madison was her sister too. She must be feeling as terrible as I was.

And then Shelby's cold, haughty mask slipped back into place. Her eyes hardened and she swept back her hair.

'I can't believe you're still so arrogant about this when it's *your* fault Madison was taken,' she sneered. 'You were supposed to be looking after her.'

Her words pierced through me. I wanted to deny them, but deep inside I knew that what she said was horribly, irrefutably true. I *had* been looking after Mo. It *was* my fault she'd been taken.

'You've totally convinced everyone the kidnapper is Sonia Holtwood,' Shelby went on, 'which means they're all terrified she'll hurt Madison, but the truth is you don't know who or what is really involved. You're out of your depth, but you've convinced Mom and Rick you're right. It's pathetic.'

'And what makes you so sure *you're* right?' I snarled, deeply stung. 'What makes you so sure that Sonia Holtwood won't just do what she said and kill Madison if we go to the police?'

A few seconds passed. Shelby's hard brown eyes bored into mine. 'That's the point,' she said icily. 'I'm saying I *don't* know which is why we should hand everything over to the cops.'

And with that, she turned and marched out of the room.

6

The Meeting Place

Dawn. I'd slept badly after the showdown with Shelby. I hadn't called Mum back, either. The last thing I needed was somebody else telling me I was getting everything wrong.

I'd been kidnapped by Sonia Holtwood myself. I'd had my life turned upside down by that woman. I knew, better than anyone, what she was capable of. And, the more I thought about it, the more convinced I was that I should stick to my gut feeling that keeping the police out of the situation was the best way to get Madison safely home.

I could hear Annie in the next room, talking in a low voice with Rick. Clearly he had spent the night here. I thought of Sam – warm, thoughtful, hard-working Sam – and felt a flush of anger on his behalf. What was Annie doing letting some muscleman she hardly knew get so close to her?

On the other hand, I had to admit that at least Rick seemed to calm her down a bit.

My phone beeped. My heart lurched as I opened the text, but it was only Mum.

Sorry didn't talk earlier. Will call u later. Hope revising going well.

I sent a short reply.

A few minutes later Annie appeared in my bedroom doorway. She glanced round. I followed her gaze to the bed. I'd laid Madison's pocket dolls across the pillow and the sight of them all lined up in their little outfits brought a lump to my throat. Tammy, the doll she'd been playing with on the beach, nestled in the centre of the group. Her shoes were still missing and her plait was still untied. I hadn't been able to bring myself to tidy her up.

Madison will do it when she comes home, I kept saying to myself. *Don't jinx things by doing it now.*

'I just came to say I'm aiming to get to the bank as soon as it opens,' Annie said in a croaky voice. Her blue eyes looked red and sore from crying.

'Would you like me to come with you?' I said, throwing back the bedcovers.

Annie offered me a shaky smile. 'Thanks, Lauren.'

Another hour dragged by. I went down to the kitchen and made some tea. I woke Jam, who had slept on the sofa in the living room, and soon after that Rick and Shelby appeared too. Rick offered to cook bacon and eggs, but none of us could manage any breakfast.

We didn't want to hang around the house – so we were all standing outside the bank when it opened. Annie went in alone to collect the cash. She emerged half an hour later with a backpack in her hand.

'I can't believe so much money fits into something so small,' she whispered.

I nodded. The bag did look tiny considering it contained two million pounds.

43

'Come on,' Rick said, looking round as he spoke. 'Let's get in the car and get back home. It's spooking me out standing here with this much cash.'

The holiday home kitchen was normally light and airy, with sunshine filtering in through the garden door and the large window over the sink. Today, however, Rick had drawn the curtains to avoid anyone in the surrounding houses peering in as Annie opened the backpack to show us the bundles of fifty-pound notes.

'I can't wait 'til that money is out of the house,' Rick muttered. 'It's giving me the heebie-jeebies having it here.'

My phone beeped.

It was *her*.

I read the text out loud:

'Tennison Bridge, North Norbourne. Eleven am. Come ALONE.'

'That's on the way to the beach where we had one of our picnics last week,' Annie said. 'D'you remember? We stopped off to take a picture.'

I nodded. The bridge had been small and pretty – made of grey stone and set over a sloping, tumbling brook. Annie had insisted on a photo of the three of us. Shelby had made a fuss, of course, but eventually we'd stood in a row and smiled. I'd been bored . . . missing my friends from London . . . missing Jam. Only Madison's chatter had cheered me up.

'How can the kidnappers be so sure we've got the money already?' Shelby said.

'They were probably following us to the bank,' Rick said.

I shivered. Then checked the time. Just over an hour to go.

'I really don't like you going on your own,' Annie said.

'The bridge is on a road,' I said. 'There'll be other cars driving past.'

'Which is weird, don't you think?' Shelby interjected. 'Why would the kidnapper risk anyone seeing what she was doing?'

'I'll be with Lauren.' Rick squeezed Annie's shoulder and she smiled gratefully up at him.

'It says *come alone.*' I pointed to the text.

'I'll stay fifty metres away,' Rick said. 'Hide behind a tree or something.'

'So will I,' Jam added.

'There's no need,' Rick said. 'I can look after Lauren.'

'And it isn't safe for you, Jam,' Annie added. 'Sonia Holtwood knows what you look like.'

'Then she'll know I'm not the police, won't she?' Jam said flatly. 'I'm going and that's that.'

Annie and Rick looked awkward, but they didn't argue. I said nothing but, inside, I felt relieved.

An hour later, Jam, Rick and I set off. Rick parked just down the road from the bridge and we got out of the car. The earth underfoot was dry and cracked. The sun was as high and bright as it had been yesterday when Madison was taken. Was that really only twenty-four hours ago? I couldn't bear to think how terrified and unhappy Madison must be, all on her own with Sonia Holtwood. The backpack containing the two million pounds felt heavy on my back. Jam took my hand.

45

I took a deep breath and sent a mental message to my little sister: *We're coming, Mo, I promise. Just hang in there* . . .

'You sure you're OK doing this?' he asked.

I nodded. Rick cleared his throat. 'I guess we should wait here,' he said gruffly. 'Lauren needs to go on alone.'

Jam met his gaze. 'No,' he said firmly. 'I'm going to wait at the bridge with her. Sonia Holtwood just said no police. And, like I said, she knows I'm not the cops, which is an advantage. Anyway, I'm not letting Lauren do this alone.'

'But she threatened to kill the little one.' Rick's voice rose in panic. 'What about the risk? Wait.'

But Jam had already dragged me away.

'You shouldn't be coming with me,' I muttered as I stumbled after him across the field towards the bridge.

I looked over my shoulder. Rick was hanging back by the car, clearly scared of following us himself.

Jam made a face. 'Like you always do what you're told.'

I bit my lip. I wanted to tell Jam I was grateful, but I didn't want to sound all mushy. Jam himself was frowning, looking round. He was clearly preoccupied with what was about to happen.

We reached the bridge. It ran over a small stream which looked like it had once been a lot bigger. We slid down the bank to the water and walked under the bridge and out the other side. There was no sign of anyone in the surrounding fields, just a couple of joggers in the distance.

A few cars passed. We waited at the bottom of the bridge,

by the stream. The sun was up now, but the air in the shade was cooler and there was a smell of damp. Rick was just visible, peering over the bonnet of his car.

'Now what?' Jam said.

I took my phone out of my pocket and checked it for what felt like the millionth time, though I knew there had been no call or text.

'We wait,' I said.

Jam nodded then strolled under the little bridge again. It was only a few metres long, but the shady side of the bridge created dense shadows. I pressed my hand against the damp stone. Despite the sparkling water, the bridge felt dank and gloomy – very different from how it had seemed last week, when we'd stopped to have our picture taken.

'This place is spooky,' I said with a shiver. 'Imagine it at night.'

As I spoke, my phone rang. *Number withheld.*

Jam stopped walking. He turned and watched as I brought the mobile to my lips.

'Hello?' I said, my voice trembling.

'Do you have the money?' It was the kidnapper's voice. Female, but disguised through that same robot-like filter. This time, though, I was sure I could make out the twang of Sonia Holtwood's American accent.

'I've got it,' I said. 'Where's Madison?'

'Safe,' Holtwood said. 'She's here. We're waiting for you.'

I looked round. There was still no sign of anyone on either side of the bridge. The joggers had long since disappeared and all I could see was an elderly man with a dog, walking slowly into the distant trees.

'Up the hill, away from the bridge and the road,' the voice went on. 'I've left the gate unlocked.'

'What gate?' I said. 'How do I know Madison's there?'

There was a scuffling noise, then the phone's filter cut out and Madison's tearful voice came on the line. 'Lauren?'

Before I could reply, the line went dead.

I froze, the mobile still in my hand.

'What did she say?' Jam was already beside me, his whisper echoing against the bridge's stone wall.

I looked around. The hill Holtwood had mentioned was to the right of the bridge, rising gently away from the road that had brought us here . . . and away from Rick.

'She wants us to go up there.' I pointed towards the incline. It led up towards a high gate in a long iron fence, surrounded by trees and shrubs.

'That looks like private land,' Jam said, uncertainly.

I shrugged. 'That's where Madison is.'

Jam and I set off up the hill. I sent Rick a text and, glancing over my shoulder, I could see he was following us at a distance.

That was reassuring, at least.

We reached the gate. It was made of rusting metal – part of an iron fence that cut through the trees and disappeared into the distance. The fence was high and topped with metal spikes set close together. It was old and rusty, for sure, but still a lethal way to keep out intruders.

'You were right,' I whispered to Jam. 'This is private property.'

'We're not the only ones who've been here.' Jam pointed to the gate, which was open a fraction.

'I guess she wants us . . . me . . . to go through.' I hesitated. I could only make out a few metres of stony path beyond the gate.

'Madison's along *there*?' Jam sounded sceptical. 'I'm not sure, Lauren, this could easily be a trap.'

'What choice do we have?' I said. 'If we don't go she'll kill Madison.' I paused. 'I know it's a risk, but I think Sonia Holtwood just wants the money. That's all she's ever wanted.'

I looked over my shoulder. Rick had reached the bridge and was watching us from there. Two cars passed along the road in quick succession.

'Rick will follow us,' I said, slightly reassured.

'OK.' Jam pushed at the iron gate.

It opened with a rusty creak.

'Let's go,' I whispered.

I followed Jam through and onto the stony path. Jam let go of the gate. We crept forwards.

Slam. The gate closed behind us with a firm click. *No.* I spun round and pushed at it, but it wouldn't budge.

Jam joined me, rattling the metal bars.

'It's locked itself,' I whispered.

'Oh, man.' Jam glanced around.

My chest constricted. Now we were locked behind the iron fence, with Rick on the other side. I could see him still

49

standing by the bridge. He clearly didn't realise we'd been locked in. Or maybe he thought he could follow us over the gate. I looked up at its high spikes and at those on the surrounding iron fence. Maybe he *could* climb over, but it wouldn't be easy.

My throat tightened. I met Jam's gaze. Should we give up and try and climb back over the gate ourselves?

I only had to think for a second. No way.

'Madison,' I said.

Jam nodded and together we set off along the path.

7

The Arrival

Despite the fierce sun it was cool on the path. Trees surrounded us on either side, casting the walkway into shade, and the damp chill of the stone seemed to seep through my sandals, into the soles of my feet. The path narrowed and we had to walk single file. I could hear the soft pad of Jam's trainers right behind me. After a moment, we came to another gate set in the long iron fence. I stood in front of it for a second, the backpack full of money still in my hand, peering out at the clearing beyond.

This was clearly the end of the private land we had walked across. Beside me, Jam pointed to the chain that was looped through the gate. It had been cut cleanly in two. Jam gave the gate a shove. It was stiffer than the one we had walked through before and dragged against the ground as we pushed it, but between us we forced it open and emerged out of the shadowy private land into the sun-washed clearing.

I shielded my eyes from the sun and looked around. We were standing in a gravel-strewn space, about fifty metres square and surrounded on all sides by trees. Four grubby maintenance vans were parked in a row at the far end, next to an iron hut. There was a rubbish tip next to the hut – mostly

51

made from broken bits of stone, as far as I could see – and scrap metal lay scattered across the ground.

Two long, winding gravel tracks led away from the clearing in opposite directions. I had no idea where we were, but it couldn't be too far from the road as traffic noises hummed in the distance.

The sun was now high in the sky, but despite the fierce heat on my head and back I still felt cold. Cold to my bones.

Where were the kidnappers? Where was Madison?

I glanced at my phone. No message. Nothing.

I tightened my grip on the backpack with the money. The handle felt sticky against my palm.

'They'll be here in a minute,' Jam said, looking round.

I thought of Rick, stuck on the other side of the gate. Had we been really stupid to come through here alone?

A white van appeared on one of the gravel paths. We stared as it drew slowly closer.

At the edge of the clearing – about fifty metres away – the van swung round so the back was now facing us. It stopped. A man got out. He was big . . . muscular, with a cap pulled down over his eyes. He walked to the rear of the van.

'You were supposed to come alone,' he called out. He had an American accent.

I said nothing. My heart was pounding in my ears.

'Marcia says to put the money there.' He pointed to a spot halfway between us, on the dusty gravel ground.

I glanced at Jam. Marcia Burns was Sonia Holtwood's real name. So she *was* behind the kidnapping. Jam said nothing, but the muscles in his jaw tightened and I knew he'd clocked the name too.

'Where's Madison?' I shouted, trying to stop my voice from shaking. 'We're not giving you anything until we've got Madison.'

The man reached for the back door of the van. He opened it slowly, keeping his eyes on Jam and me.

I gasped. Madison was inside, curled up on the floor. She struggled to her feet as the door opened, turning to face me. There was a gag round her mouth, but even from this distance I could see the terror in her huge, brown eyes. Instinctively I rushed forward, my breath catching in my throat. 'Madison!'

'Get back!' The man's yell stopped me in my tracks.

I stood, shaking, in the middle of the clearing. 'It's OK, Mo, we're here now. Are you all right?'

Madison gave me a small nod.

'You better not have hurt her!' The words exploded out of me.

The man chuckled. 'She's fine. Now bring the money over. Slowly. Put it down and we'll do the exchange.'

I walked towards the van. My legs were trembling, but I kept my gaze on Madison. She was still wearing the denim shorts and blue top from our outing to the beach. Her plaits had mostly come undone and, for some reason, it was the sight of her messy, unbrushed hair that hurt the most . . . the thought that there had been no-one to look after her . . . no-one to hold her when she cried . . .

53

'I'm going to get you,' I called out. 'Everything's going to be OK.'

Madison's hands were tied behind her with rope. I took another step forward. My legs could barely hold me up. This had to be the longest walk of my life.

'Come on!' the man shouted.

I had a flashback to the boat on which Sonia had left me to drown. This man had been with her then – his name was Frank.

The sun beat down, fierce against my face. It was almost directly overhead now, glinting off the side of the van.

'OK, Frank,' I said.

His head jerked up. He stared at me.

Good, I'd unsettled him by recognising him

Madison was now pointing at Frank as if trying to warn me about something. She twisted round, moving her fingers like she was firing a pistol. Was she trying to tell me Frank was armed? I gritted my teeth. I didn't care if he was carrying a bomb packed with enough explosives to blow up the whole of the south coast.

'I'm coming, Mo,' I called again.

'That's far enough,' Frank shouted.

I stopped, about thirty metres away from the van. I glanced over my shoulder. Jam was a little way behind me, his foot tapping nervously against the ground.

'Put down the money,' Frank ordered.

I set the backpack down in front of me. 'Let Madison go.'

Frank turned and reached inside the van. He ordered Madison to jump down. She landed with a light thud on the gravel. She started to run towards me, but Frank tripped her. She stumbled, almost losing her balance.

'You freaking bully,' I shouted. 'If you dare hurt her I'll—'

'You'll what?' Frank laughed. 'Now take a few paces back, away from the money, then I'll let the rugrat go.'

I took a step back, keeping my eyes on Madison the whole time.

'Further,' Frank ordered.

Another step. Another. Frank watched me carefully. A bead of sweat trickled down my neck.

And then the sound of an engine drifted towards us. I looked round. Through the narrow gap in the maintenance vans, I could just make out a police car shimmering in the sunshine. It was heading slowly along the gravel path behind me, a long way off still, but definitely coming towards us. As I watched, the car disappeared behind a clump of trees. It couldn't have seen us yet.

Frank stopped walking, his expression furious.

'Double-crossing little—'

In a single, swift movement he whipped a gun from his pocket. The barrel glinted in the sun. He pressed it against Madison's head.

'You told the police,' he shouted.

'No!' Panic surged up inside me. I ran forward. 'No, I didn't.'

Frank swore. 'Stop or I'll shoot her!'

I stopped running. The backpack was at my feet. A good thirty metres away from Frank and Madison.

'Throw me the money,' Frank ordered.

'Let Madison go first,' I insisted. I glanced over my shoulder. The police car was still hidden from us by the trees, but it would surely reappear again any second.

Frank swore again. Before I could move, he picked Madison up, tucked her under his arm and ran to the front of the van. Madison kicked furiously, but Frank just flung her into the front seat. A second later the engine revved and the van roared away, up the path it had come down earlier.

No. I raced after the van, a scream rising inside my throat.

But the van was roaring into the distance, leaving only whirling gravel dust behind.

Madison was gone.

8
Last Chance

Jam grabbed my arm. I hadn't even noticed him run up beside me. 'Are you OK?' he said.

My head was spinning. I couldn't think straight. I glanced round. The police car was visible again on the gravel path, driving slowly towards us. I had no idea what the police were doing here. All I could focus on was Madison, trapped in that van. A huge sob welled up in my chest. I'd promised my little sister that she'd be all right and instead I'd let her be taken away from me. Again.

The police car was almost at the end of the gravel path.

'Lauren?' Jam gripped my arm.

I took a step towards the police car. We had to get them to follow the van . . . rescue Madison.

As I moved, my phone, which was still in my hand, vibrated. *Call withheld.* It was *her.* Sonia Holtwood.

I snatched the mobile to my ear.

'Is Madison OK?' I gasped.

'What the hell are you playing at?' Sonia Holtwood – even with her voice disguised through the filter – sounded furious. 'The one thing I told you *not* to do was involve the police.'

'I didn't . . . *please.*'

'Frank *saw* the cop car.'

'I know, but *I* didn't call them. *Please*. Let me speak to Mad—'

'My gun is pointed at your sister's head right now,' Holtwood said. 'Give me one reason why I shouldn't pull the trigger.'

My whole body froze with shock. I met Jam's gaze. He looked as distraught as I felt.

Across the clearing the police car was pulling to a halt.

I looked down at the bag with the money on the ground beside me. I had to think – and move – fast. I kicked the bag across the gravel so that it was half hidden behind a large piccc of scrap metal.

'You don't have the two million,' I hissed into the phone. 'And if you shoot Madison now you'll never get it.'

'Are you threatening me?' The filtered voice hardened. 'Because you're—'

'It's not a threat,' I said, desperately. The police car front door opened and a female officer got out. 'I didn't call the cops but they're *here*. Right now.'

Holtwood sucked in her breath. 'OK, we'll do another deal,' she said quickly. 'But this is your last chance, Lauren. If you tell those officers *anything* you'll never see Madison again. Leave the phone on so I can hear.'

I took the phone away from my ear and held it in my hand.

'What's going on?' Jam hissed.

Across the clearing a male police officer had now got out of the car as well. He and the policewoman started walking towards us.

'We have to lie about the kidnapping,' I said quickly. I had no doubt Holtwood meant what she said. If she heard me speaking to the police now she would kill Madison.

'Oh, man.' Jam blew out his breath.

'Hello there.' The male police officer smiled as he reached us. He was young – not much older than we were. The woman beside him, on the other hand, was middle-aged, with grey hair and a permanent crease down the middle of her forehead.

'What are you two doing out here?' she said, unsmiling.

'We just came for a walk.' My lips were dry. 'We're not trespassing on private land, are we?'

'No.' The policewoman looked irritated. 'We had a call from a Shelby Purditt. Do you know her?'

Jam and I looked at each other. *Shelby.* So that was why the police were here.

I met the policewoman's gaze. 'Shelby's my sister.'

A beat passed. The woman was still staring at me. 'So you're *Lauren* Purditt?'

I opened my mouth. I was about to explain that my surname was different because I'd been brought up by different parents, but then I thought better of it. There was no point complicating everything.

'I'm Lauren,' I said. 'Look, I don't know what Shelby's told you, but she's always making up stuff. She does it to get me into trouble.'

Jam cleared his throat. 'What's this about?'

'The station received a call from your sister about an hour

59

ago,' the policeman said. 'She was apparently emotional and incoherent, but the gist of what she said was that your sister Madison had been kidnapped and that you were paying a two-million-pound ransom to get her back.'

Jam laughed. 'That's crazy.'

'Yeah.' I raised my eyebrows. 'Jeez, Shelby's really acting out this time.'

The young policeman fixed his eyes on my face. 'You're saying she's making her story up?'

I gripped the phone in my hand, my stomach tightening into knots.

'Of course,' I said, rolling my eyes. 'It's ridiculous. Madison's at home with our mum.'

I held my breath. Would the officers believe me? The phone in my sweating palm felt sticky.

The policewoman coughed. 'The officer on duty asked Shelby to come to the station to make a formal statement. She refused and hung up, but about ten minutes ago she called again and described where you were.' She paused. 'We were driving through the area so we came to take a look.'

I nodded, working it through in my head. When Rick couldn't get over the iron fence, he must have rung Annie who must have told Shelby what was happening . . .

'We haven't been able to get hold of Shelby's mother on the number Shelby gave us, but Shelby herself seemed convinced that when we found you, you'd be in possession of a bag containing two million pounds.' The policewoman pursed her lips. She sounded sceptical.

I shrugged, hoping she didn't notice the backpack hidden behind the large piece of scrap metal.

'As you can see, we don't have any money on us,' Jam said, holding out his empty hands to emphasise the point.

'And obviously my little sister isn't here either,' I added. The sun beat down on the back of my neck. Beads of sweat were gathering on my forehead.

'There's *no-one* else here,' Jam said. 'That's why we came.'

'Shelby makes stuff up,' I added. 'She does it all the time.'

The police officers looked at each other.

'OK,' the policewoman said. 'Well, tell your sister wasting police time is a serious issue.'

'I will,' I said.

As the police officers walked back to their car, I let out a long, shaky breath.

Beside me, Jam shook his head. 'Man, that was close,' he muttered.

I lifted my mobile to my ear again.

'Did you hear all that?' I said.

'Yes.' The filtered voice sounded calmer than before. 'Wait there. I'll call in ten minutes with instructions for the next exchange.'

She ended the call. Almost immediately my phone rang again.

'Lauren?' It was Rick. 'What the hell happened? Are you OK?'

I explained how Shelby's call to the police had resulted in the kidnap exchange going wrong.

'Where are you?' I asked.

'Trying to get round that fence with the gate you went through.' Rick swore. 'It's impossible. If you're sure you're OK, I'm going back to the bridge where I last saw you. I need to call your mum too, let her know you're all right.' He paused. 'I was thinking . . . did you notice the licence number on the van? Because if you did I could get one of my police friends to check it out. They'd do it for me as a favour, I'm sure.'

I made a face, feeling useless. I'd been so fixated on Madison it hadn't even occurred to me to check out the van's licence plate.

'I didn't look at the number,' I said. 'Did you, Jam?'

He shook his head.

'No, but the kidnapper's going to call again in a minute,' I said. 'She wants to set up another exchange.'

'Well, that's something,' Rick said. 'Where?'

'I don't know yet,' I said.

'OK.' Rick cleared his throat. 'Well, call me as soon as you know. I'll get my car and try and work out how to drive round . . . pick you guys up.'

'Thanks, Rick.' I rang off and leaned against Jam's shoulder.

'You OK, Lazerbrain?' he said softly.

I turned my head so we were facing each other. 'Not really,' I whispered.

Our lips were centimetres apart. I closed my eyes, wanting to feel the soft brush of Jam's healing kiss. But instead I felt him shifting away from me. I opened my eyes, my face

62

reddening. Jam was walking away from me, reaching for the backpack still half hidden behind the scrap metal.

I frowned, confused. Why did he not want to kiss me? With a terrible jolt it occurred to me that maybe Jam was only here, helping, because he felt he ought to. That if Madison hadn't been kidnapped he would have dumped me yesterday. I'd suspected he might be losing interest, and Shelby had said as much last night. Maybe she was right. That would explain why Jam had been distant recently. *And* why he had shied away from that kiss just now.

Jam had always wanted to kiss me before. There had to be a reason if he didn't any more.

And that was the only reason that made sense.

I closed my eyes. I couldn't think about Jam and me now. I had to keep my focus on Madison.

I tipped my face to the sun. It was still blisteringly hot. Holiday weather. Back on the beach, families were no doubt playing on the sand, just like they had yesterday.

It seemed impossible that the rest of the world was carrying on as normal, while Madison was tied up, dirty and frightened, inside Sonia Holtwood's van.

My phone rang again.

Holtwood, I mouthed at Jam as I answered.

'Lauren?' The sneering voice through the same robot-filter as before. 'Are you ready for your next instructions?'

'Where do you want to do the exchange?' I said.

'First things first,' Holtwood said smoothly. 'I told you already we are going to do another deal.'

63

'What do you mean?' I said, a chill creeping down my back, despite the fierce sun. 'There's only one deal. Madison for the money. Two million buys her freedom.'

'That's correct,' Holtwood went on. 'Except for just one thing. The price of Madison's release has just gone up.'

9

A New Deal

I stood quite still. Jam shuffled closer, trying to hear the call too.

'Lauren?' Holtwood's filtered voice on the other end of the line pierced through me. 'Are you listening?'

'Yes.' I hesitated. 'I don't understand. There isn't any more money. The insurance payment is two million pounds. Unless you want Annie to sell her house, then—'

'I'm not talking about money. I'm talking about something else, immensely valuable, hidden in Annie and Sam's London apartment.'

'*What?*' I said. My head was spinning, a million thoughts charging through me. 'There's nothing valuable at the London flat.'

'Yes, there is.' Holtwood paused. 'Your father – Sam – *said* there was.'

'*Sam* said there was?' I echoed.

What on earth was she talking about?

Jam touched my arm. *You OK?* he mouthed.

I nodded, though I wasn't in the slightest OK.

'Sam's exact words on what he'd hidden were: "*there is something of huge value*",' Holtwood said. 'D'you hear that? *Something of huge value*. That's got to mean big money.'

'I don't understand,' I went on. 'Why would Sam have hidden something valuable in a flat he hardly ever used, in a city he hardly ever visited?'

'Because the valuable thing is for you, Lauren . . . and you *do* live in that city.'

My chest constricted. 'For me?'

'Yes, I don't know what it is, but he was planning to give it to you next time he saw you.'

'How do you know all this?' I said. 'How do you know what Sam's "exact words" were?'

'Never mind that,' Holtwood said sharply. 'You need to go to the apartment immediately. It's almost midday now. If you walk along the track where the van drove earlier you'll come to a town called Ringbourne. The next train for London leaves in twenty minutes. I'll give you two hours from now to get to the apartment. Then another two to find whatever is hidden there.'

'No,' I gasped. 'Wait. That isn't enough time. I don't even know what I'm looking for.'

'Then you better get started,' Holtwood snapped. 'One more thing. Under no circumstances are you to tell anyone else where you're going. Especially Annie and that man she's with.'

'Why not?' I said. 'Why not tell Annie?'

'Surely you can work that out, can't you, Lauren?' Holtwood sneered. 'I'll call again at four.' She rang off.

I gulped.

'What's going on, Lauren?' Jam asked. 'I could only hear bits of that.'

I told him what Holtwood had said.

Jam frowned. 'How could Sonia Holtwood possibly know about Sam hiding something valuable for you in the London flat?'

'I don't know,' I said. 'The point is she's not letting Madison go unless we find whatever it is.'

Jam shook his head. 'Maybe we should call Rick?' he said. 'I'm sure when he understands how important it is, he'll drive us to London.'

'No.' I stared past Jam towards the rubbish heap full of broken stones. I had a sudden flashback to the beach and how I'd watched the ice cream vendor leaning forward to hear Madison's order. Though I hadn't been able to see her face I was sure she would have smiled up at him, just as she had smiled at me, moments before. And now she was in the back of a van, separated from everyone she loved and who loved her.

I couldn't bear it. I had to get her back – and as fast as possible. Whatever it took.

'Sonia Holtwood said not to tell Annie or Rick.' I hesitated. 'Maybe . . . maybe she thinks Annie doesn't want me to have whatever it is . . . maybe Annie's been deliberately keeping this valuable thing away from me.'

Jam frowned. 'I don't believe Annie would do that,' he said. 'Especially now, with Madison's life at stake.'

'Yeah?' My heart felt like ice.

'Yes, and I also think Annie has a right to know what's going on,' he said stubbornly. 'You'd want to know if the situation was reversed.'

'But Annie's crazy,' I said. 'Maybe she's better off not knowing all the details. She can't handle stuff like I can. In fact, she and I don't do *anything* the same.'

'You both love Madison,' Jam persisted.

We stared at each other.

'I'm right about this,' I said. 'I *know* I am. We have to go to London and find out what Sam hid there. And we have to keep quiet about it to Annie and Rick.'

Jam shook his head. 'Man, you always think you're right, don't you?'

'No,' I said. 'But I'm right about this.'

Jam checked his watch. 'So how are we going to get to London?' he said.

I indicated the track ahead of us. 'According to Holtwood, that leads to a town where we can get a train.'

Jam stared at me. 'I don't have enough money for a train ticket.'

'Me neither, but it's fine.' I pointed to the backpack. 'There's two million in there. We'll use a bit of that. If there's really something amazingly valuable hidden in the London house, a few quid out of this won't make any difference.'

Jam's face split into a smile. 'Not only always right, but also insane,' he said.

I grinned back, my stomach cartwheeling in spite of my fears for Madison and for what we were about to do. Even after all the time I'd known him, Jam's smile still made me melt. Then I thought back to how he'd pulled away from my kiss.

The smile fell from my face. Again, I wondered . . . was he just helping me because he thought he ought to?

'What?' Jam's eyes filled with confusion. 'What's up now?'

His phone beeped before I could say anything. He glanced at the text, then shoved the mobile away.

'Who was that?' I could hear the sharp edge in my voice and hated myself for letting my vulnerability show.

What did it matter what Jam thought or did? I was strong. If it came down to it I could survive without him.

'It was Mum asking when I'll be home.' Jam rolled his eyes. 'The usual.'

'Right.' We headed along the track but, as we walked, doubt crept through me. Was that really Jam's mum? Or was it some other girl he didn't want me to know about?

We walked into Annie and Sam's London flat in Notting Hill at 1.40 pm. Though Annie had given me a key that I always kept on my key ring, I hadn't been inside since Sam died, and the memories of him were overwhelming.

The main room was large and open-plan, with a kitchen area at one end. There was the soft, cream sofa Sam used to lie on, laptop in front of him, his forehead creased in a frown of concentration, working until Annie nagged him to stop. He used to wink at me sometimes when she got upset, as if to say: *I know she's emotional, but we can handle her*. For a moment, I felt a surge of anger with Sam for not being here. He would never have gone to pieces, like Annie. If he were around he'd know exactly how to handle the kidnappers.

69

'Where on earth do we start?' Jam said, glancing around.

I gulped. The flat was neat and tidy – and it wasn't large – but we were still facing an uphill struggle. I checked the time again. Sonia Holtwood had given us until 4 pm to search the entire apartment for anything valuable. That deadline was only just over two hours away. For the first time since Madison disappeared I felt totally isolated. I'd texted Annie from our train, reassuring her that Jam and I were fine and explaining in vague terms that we were following the kidnapper's instructions for the next attempt at a handover. But Annie didn't know about our two-hour deadline. Neither did Rick.

'I don't know where to start looking,' I said, sinking into one of the sofas.

'Well, I'm gonna try here.' Jam opened the cupboard under the TV.

I glanced through the window to the small balcony which was the only outside space in the flat. Sam and Annie had bought the flat partly as an investment for me . . . somewhere for me to one day inherit. I had a sudden flashback to being here with Madison last year. We'd chatted on that very balcony about how one day we would live here, together – with me working and Madison maybe at college in London.

My insides seemed to shrivel up. Up until Madison's disappearance I had been so sure she'd be in my life forever. And now, here I was, facing a possible future without her.

'This is hopeless,' I said.

Across the room, Jam stood up. 'Giving up so soon?' He raised an eyebrow.

Was he sneering at me?

'No, I'm not,' I snapped. 'You stay here. I'll check out the bedrooms.'

I strode across the hallway and up the stairs. There were two bedrooms in the flat, each with their own bathroom. Annie and Sam used to sleep in one, with Madison in a fold-out bed by the wardrobe. Shelby and I were supposed to share the other room, though in practice Shelby hadn't visited the flat much in the short time Annie and Sam had owned it. When they came to visit, she tended to stay behind with friends in the States. I headed for Annie and Sam's room, opened the sliding door of the long, wooden wardrobe and pulled out an armful of shoeboxes.

My phone rang. I jumped, but it was only Mum. I let the call go to voice mail. I knew what the message would say without even listening to it: *hope you are revising . . . call me . . .* I wrote a quick text back saying I would ring later.

As I pressed send, I heard a scuffing noise outside the room. I looked up. There it was again. The sound of a hand trailing along the wall up the stairs. Was that Jam, following me up here?

'Jam?' I called out.

No reply.

I froze, as whoever it was reached the top of the stairs. Footsteps sounded across the short landing. Then stopped.

I tensed, my pulse racing. I looked round, desperately, for something . . . anything . . . I could use as a weapon. An open

71

shoebox lay at my feet. I grabbed the shoe inside – an elegant stiletto of Annie's – and clutched it in my hand.

'Who's there?'

Again, no reply.

I stood, arm raised, as the door creaked slowly open.

10

Revelations

The door opened fully. I held my breath, my heart pounding. Shelby stood in the doorway, her mouth in an 'o' shape of shock.

'You?' I stared at her, lowering the stiletto. 'What are you doing here?'

Shelby glanced at the shoeboxes lying open at my feet. 'Why are you going through Mom's stuff?' she demanded.

No way was I going to take that accusing tone from her.

'Why did you call the police?' I snapped back. 'What were you thinking? Madison could have been killed.'

Shelby met my gaze. 'Don't lecture me about Madison. It's *your* fault she was taken in the first place.' She paused. 'Anyway, you haven't answered my question. Why are you here?'

'I'm looking for something,' I said as icily as I could.

'In Mom's closet?' Shelby raised her eyebrows.

I hesitated. Jam and I were up against a deadline here – so we could certainly use Shelby's help – but how could I trust her after she'd gone to the police earlier?

'I'm sorry, but it's none of your business,' I said.

'It is so, you toxic cow.'

My mouth gaped. She was *unbelievable*.

Shelby put her hands on her hips. She was wearing cut-off jeans that did nothing for her rather short, stumpy legs. Her hair was unbrushed and pulled unattractively off her face in a loose ponytail and, as usual, her make-up was far too heavy.

I wanted to point out all of these things. I wanted to hurt her. But I bit back the scathing words that were itching to leap out of my mouth. I *had* to focus on Madison.

'We can talk about who's toxic when Madison's home,' I said calmly. 'Right now I'm concentrating on rescuing her. Maybe you could do the same.'

Shelby's lip curled with fury. 'What has getting Madison back got to do with you poking around in Mom's closet?'

'I told you to mind your own business,' I snapped. 'You already ruined one exchange by running to the police. Luckily for you Mo's all right, but if they'd killed her it would be your fault so I'm not telling you anything about what they want us to do now.'

'Is Madison really OK?' Shelby's voice lost its harsh edge. 'Mom showed me your text, but . . . did you speak to her?'

'Like you care.'

Shelby's lip trembled. She turned to walk away and bumped into Jam who just then appeared in the doorway.

'Hey, Shelbs, I didn't hear you come in.' He frowned. 'You come to help with the search?'

Shelby blushed. 'Lauren doesn't want me to.'

Jam glanced over at me. 'That's stupid, Lazerbrain. We don't have much time, we should use all the help we can get.'

74

Anger rose inside me. How dare Jam side with Shelby?

'How did you know where we were?' Jam turned back to Shelby.

'This.' Shelby held out her phone to him.

Jam took in whatever was on the screen and looked up at me.

'She's had a text from the kidnappers, Lauren,' he said. 'Telling her the same as you.'

'What?' I said. 'Why didn't you say so?'

Shelby shrugged. 'They just told me to come and search the flat for some valuable thing Dad left me,' she said.

A wave of jealousy washed over me.

I hated myself for it. After all, finding and rescuing Madison was what really mattered – but it wasn't fair. Shelby had been Sam's daughter all her life. I'd only really known him for a year before he died. If he'd left both of us something then it wasn't specially for me.

'So if you knew about these supposed valuables then you already *knew* what I was looking for?' I glared at her.

Honestly, she was impossible.

Shelby gave me a sulky look back.

'I'm surprised you haven't shown that text from the kidnappers straight to the police,' I said, acid in my voice.

'How did you get here?' Jam asked.

'I took the train, same as you,' Shelby explained.

'Annie'll be worried sick,' I said reproachfully.

'She thinks I've gone out for the afternoon with a friend visiting from home. Rick persuaded her to let me go. Said I

75

needed the break. Anyway . . .' Shelby looked away. 'Mom's mad at me for calling the police.'

'Your mum's just upset because of Madison.' Jam patted Shelby's arm. 'It's not your fault.'

Shelby smiled gratefully at him. 'I feel real bad about all that,' she said in a low voice.

'You mean you admit you were wrong to go to the cops?' I said.

Shelby pressed her lips together, her face mutinous. 'I'm not saying that,' she said.

Jam rolled his eyes. 'May I remind you both that we have very little time to find out if there's anything valuable here, so maybe we should get on with it?'

Jealousy rose inside me again. It was one thing Jam telling me off when we were alone. But it was humiliating to do it in front of Shelby.

'Fine,' I said, not making eye contact with either of them. 'Why don't you take the other bedroom, Shelby? I'll carry on looking in here.'

'Whatever.' Shelby disappeared from view.

Jam was still standing in the doorway, but I turned my attention to the pile of boxes at my feet. I sensed him waiting there for a few seconds, but when I finally looked up he was gone.

I tried to lose myself in the search – to put my anxiety about Madison, my irritation with Jam and my dislike of Shelby all out of my mind.

As I systematically pored over every inch of the wardrobe, my brain was still working at ninety miles an hour. I didn't

76

understand why the kidnappers had suddenly decided to involve Shelby. Maybe they thought approaching her directly would make her think twice about blabbing to the police again. Or maybe they'd always intended to involve us both if the original exchange failed.

I couldn't work it out.

There was definitely nothing in the wardrobe. It wasn't full – just a few dresses and coats of Annie's at one end – and some of Sam's polo shirts and jeans at the other. This wasn't surprising, of course. Annie and Sam only bought the apartment in order to have a base to stay in when they visited me in London.

I found an old leather jacket of Sam's in the far corner, where it had fallen off its hanger. I searched its pockets, which were empty, then pressed it to my face.

The lemony scent of Sam's aftershave filled my nostrils, cutting through the dense smell of the leather. I suddenly hurt with the loss of him. Aside from Madison, I'd always got on better with Sam than with anyone else in my birth family. He was far more laid-back than Annie – kind and sweet with Madison and he always treated me as a grown-up.

I put the jacket on a hanger and placed it carefully back on the rail. I rummaged through a pile of jumpers, two drawers of underwear and a stack of CDs.

There was nothing here of any value, as far as I could see.

I turned to the rest of the room. I could hear Shelby banging about in the bedroom opposite. Jam was silent downstairs.

Sighing, I crossed the room to the first of the two bedside drawers. One was full of clutter: a stack of romance novels, a nail file, some eyelash curlers and two tubes of hand cream.

Guessing this was Annie's side of the bed, I crawled over the duvet to the other. Everything was clean and dusted – Annie must pay a cleaner to come in regularly. The second bedside drawer was neater, simply containing a bundle of bank statements, a few receipts and some yacht magazines. Definitely Sam's stuff.

I sat on the bed and pored over the papers. Weird to think Sam must have been the last person to touch them, just shoving them in this little drawer and imagining he would one day soon come back to them. There was nothing of any value in here. Even the bank statements only referred to relatively tiny amounts of cash – just a few hundred quid going in and out over several months.

I put the papers back in the drawer. But I couldn't lay them flat. There was something right at the end of the drawer. I felt inside and drew out a small metal box. It was locked and there was no sign of a key.

I hesitated, then shook the box. Nothing rattled or clinked. Whatever was inside must be well padded. It could easily be jewellery – or cash.

I had to find out what was there. Grabbing one of the nail files from the other bedside drawer, I prised open the lid.

Two white envelopes lay inside.

I picked them up. They were flat and light – no bulky objects inside.

One envelope was addressed to Shelby, the other to me. Neither was properly sealed.

I laid Shelby's envelope on the bed and picked up mine. With trembling hands, I unfolded the piece of paper inside: one side of A4, in Sam's elegant handwriting.

Dear Lauren

What I have just told you will have come as a shock but now you are old enough to know the truth. I never wanted to lie but Annie thought it was for the best and – once you had been taken from us – the decision was out of our hands.

I am writing this letter so that the facts are down on paper, for you to come back to once the initial shock has worn off.

My heart thumped. Clearly Sam had written this letter assuming I would read it after a conversation that, thanks to his death, had never taken place. I read on.

I'm always happy to talk about what we did and why. This letter is not a substitute for any future conversations, just an attempt to offer some clarity. I hope you will understand.

As you now know, you are not my biological daughter.

I stopped reading. *What?* It couldn't be true. Every cell in my body screamed out against the words on the page.

Sam wasn't my birth dad?

How could that *possibly* be true? Everything I'd done two years ago to find Annie and Sam had been based on needing to know who my real parents were. And I had found them. It had taken a flight to America and a bus ride through Vermont after which I'd been lied to, kidnapped and left for dead in a desolate, snow-laden forest . . . but I had found them. My birth mum and dad.

And now, my father . . . my *second* father was telling me he wasn't my birth dad *either*?

Still barely able to take it in, I read on.

I was unable to have my own children. Annie and I knew this three years into our marriage, after a year of trying for a baby and a series of fertility tests. The sperm donor did not legally have to give his name and Annie and I know nothing about him, other than that he was a medical student with colouring as close to mine as we could manage. We had to explain this to the police and the FBI, of course, when we were required to undergo DNA testing to prove we were your parents. It was easy to produce the sperm donor paperwork to show the true circumstances of your conception and those involved were extremely sympathetic. More than anything, we didn't want to overload you with information when you were already having to adjust to us as your birth parents.

I stopped reading again. Annie and Sam had lied over my DNA test? It felt like the world as I knew it had been turned on its head.

Shelby's father is another story. By now I imagine you girls will have confided in each other and she will know her heritage as you know yours. I know you will do your best to help her with the inevitable pain she will experience. Hers is a heavy burden to carry.

Madison is still very young and I'm not sure she is ready to learn that she was conceived through the same sperm donor as you. Perhaps we could discuss that? I'm happy to give you any further information I can, though I have to stress the donor sperm we used was from an anonymous hospital source. He has no idea of your existence and we know nothing about him.

Please believe that I could not love you more if you had been born from my blood. I hope you will feel able to talk to me and Annie about all this but, however you respond, we will always be your loving parents.

Sam

My mind reeled. This was too much . . . too overwhelming to cope with. I shoved the letter in my pocket. How could Sam and Annie have kept this huge piece of information from me?

Not just me. Shelby's letter, lying unopened on the bed, caught my eye. I picked it up and glanced towards the bedroom opposite. I could hear her in there, banging drawers and cursing.

I stared down at the envelope in my hand. If Sam couldn't have his own kids and Madison and I were the product of a sperm donor then who on earth was Shelby's dad?

I know you will do your best to help her with the inevitable pain she will experience. Hers is a heavy burden to carry.

Sam's words careered around my head. The way things were between Shelby and me, I couldn't see her asking for my help over anything.

Which meant Shelby dealing with whatever was in this letter on her own.

That wasn't right.

And it wasn't what Sam wanted.

No, if I was really going to help Shelby I needed to know what 'heavy burden' Sam had been talking about.

I hesitated for only a second, then I took out Shelby's letter.

What I read shocked me to the core.

11

The Boy

I was so caught up in what I was reading that I didn't hear Jam come into the room until he sat down on the other side of the bed.

I looked up. 'Oh, Jam.'

'I haven't found anything,' he said. 'What are you doing?'

'You're not going to believe this,' I whispered.

He frowned. 'What?'

I opened my mouth to speak, but it was hard. I still couldn't quite believe it was true and saying it would make it real.

'*What?*' Jam said impatiently.

I handed him the letter addressed to me.

'None of us are really Sam's kids,' I whispered.

I turned back to Shelby's letter. Much of it was written in a similar style and expressing similar feelings as my own. Again, it assumed an important conversation had already taken place and stressed how proud Sam was of her. But one paragraph stood out.

Your mother was finding it hard to be a full-time mom to your older sister and still struggling with the fact that I wasn't able to give her a child. We even separated for a while under the pressure. The affair just happened, Shelby, it was one of those things. Your mom was vulnerable. Simeon Duchovny, as I know she will have explained, represented a different world. She never stopped loving me and neither of us have ever loved you any the less because of the circumstances in which you were conceived.

I read it again. Shelby was the product of an affair. Annie had slept with someone else. Some other man – not Sam and not the anonymous sperm donor who'd fathered me and Madison – was Shelby's actual dad.

I couldn't take it in. And yet it made sense. Shelby looked so different from me and Madison. Her colouring was different . . . and her body shape. And it was certainly easy to imagine neurotic, emotional Annie finding it impossible to cope with life and running away from her responsibilities for a while.

It all fitted.

'This is heavy.' Jam looked up, his eyes full of shock. 'Sam *isn't* your birth dad?'

I pressed my finger to my lips and handed him Shelby's letter. 'Or Shelby's,' I whispered.

Jam's eyes widened as he read. 'Oh, man,' he breathed. He looked up and shook his head. 'This is addressed to Shelby,' he said quietly. 'We shouldn't be reading it.'

I stared at him. 'I know, but—'

Jam turned away. 'I'll give it to her.'

'No!' I reached across the bed and grabbed the letter off him. 'Wait a sec.'

'Lauren, it's not your decision. Sam wanted her to know.'

'Well, I bet Annie didn't,' I whispered. 'In fact, I bet Annie doesn't even know these letters are here.'

'Well, they aren't *from* Annie, they're from Sam, and—'

'That's not what I mean,' I said. 'It's just that this is a *huge* deal . . .'

Jam raised his eyebrows. 'D'you think I don't know that? That's why we have to—'

'I just think we should wait,' I whispered. 'Think about it. Shelby's already upset about Madison. Her dad only died last year. She hates me. And now this . . .' I pointed to the letter. 'Of course she has to know, but if we show her now she'll have, like, *total* hysterics. We've got to stay focused on getting Madison back . . . which means we have to keep looking for the things Sam hid.'

'What are you talking about?' Jam looked at me as if I were mad. 'Where did you find these letters?'

I pointed to the little metal box. 'They were locked in there,' I said.

'Don't you get it?' Jam hissed. 'These letters *are* the things Sam hid. I mean, you had to break into that box to get them out. And Holtwood said the words he'd used about what he'd hidden were: *something of huge value*. Well, what could be of more "value" to Sam than letters telling you and Shelby the truth about your parentage after so many years?'

'Wait.' My head was spinning, trying to take in what he

was saying. 'Even if Sam saw a value in the letters, they still aren't worth any money. The kidnappers won't be interested . . . jeez, what are we going to tell them? What's going to happen to Madison?'

'I don't know,' Jam said, 'but I'm going to let Shelby know about her letter anyway.'

'No,' I persisted. 'Not *now*. We *have* to make finding Madison the priority right now. Showing Shelby . . . it's not the right thing to do.'

'Here we go again.' Jam's eyes hardened. 'You always know what the right thing to do is, don't you, Lauren?'

'That's not fair. *Please*, Jam.'

Jam hesitated, his hand on the door handle.

At that moment, Shelby appeared. She stared suspiciously at me. 'What's going on?' she said. 'Have you found anything?'

Jam was still holding Shelby's letter in his hand. She hadn't noticed. All her focus was on me.

'Just a bunch of papers.' I indicated the pile I'd taken from the bedside drawer earlier. The magazines were still strewn across the bed. The open metal box, now empty, lay on top.

Shelby groaned. 'There's nothing valuable in this place,' she said. 'Maybe Sonia Holtwood was wrong.'

Jam looked over at me. I could see the struggle in his eyes.

I offered a silent prayer. *Please, Jam.*

With a sigh, Jam slid Shelby's letter into his jeans pocket. 'Yes,' he said. 'Maybe Sonia Holtwood was wrong.'

'Which means we have to find another way of getting

Madison back.' I stood up. 'We're going to have to track her down ourselves.'

Shelby and Jam stared at me.

'How?' Shelby said.

'Where would we start?' Jam added.

'Well, we know she's been taken by Sonia Holtwood whose real name is Marcia Burns. And we know the guy who is helping her is Frank, who she worked with two years ago when they took me and Madison on the boat.'

'How does that help?' Shelby asked. 'Knowing who they are doesn't mean we know *where* they are.'

'But it means we can describe them,' I said. 'When it comes to Sonia, we can easily find pictures if we look online. Maybe there'll be a photo of Frank from the trial too.'

Jam nodded. 'OK, but who do we ask? Madison just vanished from the beach . . . you said no-one you spoke to had seen her – or seen anyone with her.'

This was true. I frowned, thinking back to the moments just before Madison had gone missing. I'd been watching her all the way to the ice cream kiosk. I hadn't taken my eyes off her, until . . .

'There was a boy.' My pulse quickened as the memory – and what it meant – fell into place. 'A boy on the beach. He came up to me just, like, seconds before Madison disappeared,' I said.

'So what?' Shelby said.

'He deliberately distracted me,' I said, thinking it through and realising it was true. 'He came right up to me and asked me if I knew some girl called Cassie.'

'Who's Cassie?' Shelby asked.

'No-one. That's the point. I'm sure he was just trying to get my attention, so I wouldn't notice if someone approached Madison.'

'But why would a random boy on the beach *do* that?' Shelby frowned.

I shook my head. 'I don't know.'

'OK.' Jam rubbed at his forehead. 'OK, well, we need to track this boy down and find out.'

'How will we track him down?' Shelby asked. 'Just because he was on the beach on Monday . . . he could be anywhere now.'

'He was wearing a Boondog Shack T-shirt, so maybe he works there. I saw him later, outside the Boondog,' I said, remembering. 'He was chatting to a group of people. He looked like the sort of person who'd be popular. Someone might remember him there.'

Jam looked at me sideways. Was he wondering why I'd paid this guy quite so much attention? I blushed, remembering how good-looking the boy had been.

'What's the Boondog Shack?' Jam asked.

'It's a surfer-style café,' I explained. 'Near the beach. Teenagers hang out there.'

Shelby nodded. 'I went down there every day last week.'

Really? 'I didn't know that,' I said.

She shrugged. 'What else was I gonna do? Stay home with Mom? You and Madison were off doing stuff together all the time. I didn't have much choice.'

'You know, Shelby, if there's a college that does a degree course in whining you'll get in, no problem,' I snapped.

Shelby threw me a fierce look.

'Lauren, please.' Jam glared at me, then checked his watch. 'It's almost 2 pm. Holtwood's calling again at 4. What are we going to tell her?'

'We'll tell her we need more time,' I said, feeling nettled. Why did Jam have to behave as if *I* was the one in the wrong. Shelby was the snitch who'd gone behind our backs to the police and stopped us getting Madison back. 'We'll tell Holtwood we're still in London, looking for whatever Sam hid.'

Jam looked sceptical. 'But instead we're going to Norbourne? We're going to attempt to find some surfer boy who may or may not know something?' He paused. 'It's not much of a lead, is it?'

'It's all we've got,' I said.

'Come on, then,' Shelby said.

'Not you,' I said. 'You can come back with us to Norbourne, but you're not helping us look for Mo.'

'Why not?' Shelby said indignantly.

'Because I don't trust you.' I put my hands on my hips.

Honestly, how could Shelby expect us to include her when she had betrayed us just hours before?

'That's not fair,' Shelby said. 'I want Madison back as much as you.'

I opened my mouth to tell her that I sincerely doubted that, but before I could speak, Jam patted his jeans pocket . . . the one containing Sam's letter to Shelby.

'Lauren,' he said, a warning tone to his voice, 'I think we should let Shelby help if she wants to.'

I bit my lip, resentment mingling with fear that if I didn't agree Jam would show Shelby the letter and then all hell would break loose and we'd be further away than ever from finding Madison.

'Fine,' I said.

Shelby smiled triumphantly and marched out of the room.

Jam shouldered the backpack with the two million and turned to me. 'Thanks, Lauren.' He lowered his voice. 'You know, I can think of a lot better things to spend money on than cross-country train journeys and insane treasure hunts.'

'Yeah?' I felt for the wooden oval on its string round my neck. 'Well, I guess that's what you get if you go out with me.'

I smiled, hoping Jam would smile that crinkly smile of his back at me, but he just rolled his eyes and headed after Shelby.

I picked Sam's letter to me off the bed, folded and pocketed it and followed them. What with everything else going on, the knowledge he wasn't my biological dad hadn't begun to sink in. It didn't feel real. Which was fine – worrying about that stuff was the last thing I needed right now.

We got back to Norbourne in record time and made straight for the Boondog Shack. The place was buzzing. I'd only seen it from a distance before, but it was cool. A great track was playing, there was nobody in there over twenty-one and the staff were all fit and very smiley.

A couple of the waiters recognised Shelby and threw her a wave. She looked extremely pleased with herself as she led the way to a table by the window.

I described the boy who'd spoken to me on the beach to our waitress. 'I think he knows someone called Cassie who comes here?' I said, remembering the name the boy had asked about.

The waitress said she didn't know either of them. It was the same with the next two waiters I asked. I checked the time. Holtwood was due to ring me in twenty minutes.

It was starting to look like we'd made a terrible mistake in coming here. And then a girl with curly brown hair and freckles beckoned me over. She'd been sitting close to the door, watching me ask the waiters if they knew the blond boy. I'd described him as tall and good-looking, trying to ignore the quizzical look Jam had given me when I did so.

I left Jam and Shelby still chatting to the waiters and went over to the girl with the freckles.

'The boy you're looking for?' she said with a frown. 'Why d'you want to find him?'

I hesitated. The freckly girl knew him . . . that was obvious . . . and she didn't look that thrilled to be talking about him. But I didn't get the impression she was annoyed with me for asking – if anything she seemed sympathetic.

I took a deep breath. 'He asked me out,' I lied. 'Told me to meet him here.'

Freckles raised her eyebrows. 'He's *such* a loser.'

'Yeah?' I said. 'So . . . so does he work here or not?'

Freckles shook her head sorrowfully. 'He just hangs out

here. Right now he's with his latest girlfriend.' She pointed through the Shack's window, towards a restaurant further along the promenade. 'They'll be in there.'

'Thanks.' I turned away.

Freckles grabbed my arm. 'Don't waste your time on him,' she said. 'I wish I hadn't.'

We hurried out of the Shack and along the promenade. As we neared the carousel, the faint strains of its usual music drifted towards us – a brass band version of 'The Teddy Bear's Picnic'. It had been playing the same tune when Madison and I had walked past . . . was that really only a day ago?

We left the carousel behind and headed towards the restaurant. It was a large pizza place filled with customers.

I spotted the boy as soon as I walked in. He was leaning back in his booth, clearly flirting with the heavily-lipsticked girl sitting opposite him. I checked the time. 3.45 pm. Sonia Holtwood would be calling in fifteen minutes. What on earth was I going to say to her?

This boy *had* to have some information.

He looked up as Jam, Shelby and I walked over. His face was as chiselled and model-like as I remembered, though he showed no sign of recognising me.

'Hi.' He looked from me to Shelby to Jam. 'Did you want something?'

'You came up to me on the beach yesterday,' I said. 'You asked if I knew a girl called Cassie.'

The boy's eyes widened. *Now* he was remembering. I could see it.

92

'Who's Cassie?' the pink-lipsticked girl opposite him said suspiciously. She looked at me. 'Who are you?'

'My name's Lauren.' I turned back to the boy. 'All I want to know is who told you to speak to me.'

'No-one told me to,' the boy said.

'Yes, they did,' Shelby said.

'I bet they paid you to do it too,' Jam added shrewdly.

'What is all this?' whined Lipstick Girl. 'What's going on, Matt?'

Matt stood up, a lock of blond hair falling over his forehead.

'Go away,' he said viciously.

We glared at each other. He was a lot taller than me. Taller even than Jam. But I stood my ground.

'The people who paid you have kidnapped our sister,' I said, lowering my voice so the girl at the table couldn't hear. 'They're capable of killing her. They *will* kill her if we don't find her first.'

Matt's tanned, handsome face paled.

'If you don't help us I'll tell the police you were helping the kidnappers. That'll make you an accessory to a serious crime.'

'No.' Matt gulped. 'Don't go to the police. I—'

'. . . already have a record?' Jam suggested.

Matt frowned with anxiety. 'It was a woman,' he said, his voice barely audible. 'She didn't give me her name, but she had an American accent.'

'Holtwood,' Shelby breathed.

'OK,' I said 'Tell me everything that happened.'

12

The Trail

Matt led us away from his table. Lipstick Girl frowned, but didn't attempt to follow. Matt stopped beside a glass cupboard containing shelves of cakes and desserts, then spoke in a low voice.

'The woman who came up to me was older . . . maybe in her forties, and American . . . I dunno,' he said. 'She was wearing a cap, pulled down low, and shades. Didn't say her name. Just paid me a hundred pounds to walk up to you on the beach and distract you . . . I don't really know anyone called Cassie. I made that up.'

He brushed his blond curls off his forehead and glanced quickly round the restaurant as if to check no-one had over-heard him.

'How did this woman find you?' I asked.

Matt shrugged. 'I was hanging outside the Boondog,' he said. 'She came up to me, asked if I wanted to earn some cash.'

'Didn't you ask why?' Jam said.

'Weren't you suspicious?' Shelby added.

'No. Look, it was all over in, like, ten minutes. She turned up here, took me over to the carousel place by the beach, gave me the money and told me when to walk over to you.'

I looked through the pizza restaurant window. Though I couldn't hear the music from here, the carousel was clearly visible – a moving circle of prancing ponies. When Madison and I had walked past it on the morning she'd gone missing, Sonia Holtwood must have been standing there watching us. I shivered.

'Matty, what's going on?' Lipstick Girl came over, hands on hips.

Matt threw an appealing glance at me. 'We're done, aren't we?'

'In a sec.' Jam quickly fished his phone out of his pocket. He held out a picture of Sonia Holtwood we'd found earlier. It was the best one we could get our hands on, but I knew Holtwood was easily capable of changing her appearance. 'Is this the woman you spoke to?'

Matt looked at the photo, then shook his head.

'Maybe but, like I said, she was in a cap and shades, so it's hard to tell.'

'OK.' Jam took his phone.

Matt went back to his table.

My heart sank. Matt had been our only lead to Madison and – despite what he'd told us – we'd reached a dead end.

'Now what?' Shelby turned to me, her eyes wide with fear. 'Sonia Holtwood's going to call you any moment and we're no closer than we were before to finding Madison.'

I bit my lip.

'Man, she's going to expect you to have something to add to the ransom,' Jam said. 'What are you going to tell her?'

'I don't know.' Feeling sick, I led the others outside and onto the promenade. It wasn't quite as busy as yesterday, the Easter Monday bank holiday, but the beach was still full of families enjoying the heat wave.

I tried to focus on the options. It was hard to think straight. The image of Madison in the back of that van kept forcing itself into my mind's eye. 'Holtwood thinks we're still in London,' I said. 'Maybe I can use that.'

'How?' Shelby asked.

My phone rang.

I glanced at Jam. He gave me a swift, encouraging nod. I hurried into a gap between two stalls and cupped my hand over my mobile as I brought it to my mouth. I didn't want Holtwood to hear the sounds of the seaside around me.

'Hello?' I said.

'Lauren.' The same, disguised, voice as before.

'You might as well skip the filter,' I said. 'I know you're Sonia Holtwood.'

'Have you found whatever Sam hid?'

The contents of the two letters flashed into my mind. Sam wasn't my biological father. Or my sisters'. *Stop it, Lauren.* I couldn't let myself get distracted.

I also couldn't admit the truth.

'We need more time to find whatever it is,' I lied.

A pause. The line crackled in the silence.

'More time isn't acceptable,' Holtwood said. 'I told you what would happen to Madison if you didn't come through.'

My stomach gave a sick lurch. I *had* to buy us more time. It was the only way to stop Holtwood carrying out her threat.

'How do I know you haven't killed Madison already?' I said.

The crackle on the line stopped. For a second I could hear background sounds quite clearly: a few notes of music – strangely familiar – then some distant, excited shrieks . . . and then Madison's voice in my ear.

'Lauren, are you there?'

'Yes, sweetheart I'm—'

'Enough.' The filter re-engaged and Holtwood's snarling voice came back on the line. 'You're out of time,' she snapped.

'Wait, we've almost finished searching the flat,' I insisted, trying to keep my voice strong. 'We just need a bit more time.'

Another pause. 'I will give you another twenty minutes,' Holtwood said. 'But we're finishing this tonight, one way or another.'

The line went dead.

'What happened?' Jam said.

My voice sounded like someone else's – dull and flat – as I explained. 'We've got twenty minutes,' I finished.

'What about Madison? Was she there?' Shelby asked.

I nodded. 'And there was this music . . .' I stopped. I was certain I'd heard those notes somewhere before – but *where*?

Shelby's eyes widened. 'So . . . if we don't think of something in the next twenty minutes then Holtwood will kill Madison?'

I nodded again. What on earth were we going to do?

'Maybe Mom will know about something else valuable?' Shelby suggested excitedly.

'I doubt it,' I said, heavily. 'I mean, between us we know what she owns and there's hardly anything worth more than a few hundred dollars.'

'What about her jewellery?' Shelby said.

'OK, but it's not worth millions. Holtwood's looking for "big money" stuff. That's what she said.'

'We can still try,' Shelby said.

'She's right, Lauren,' Jam said.

'OK.' I couldn't see how turning to Annie at this point would help at all – but I had no alternative suggestion.

We raced along the promenade towards the carousel. The turning for the holiday home was just past it. This was the same route I'd taken yesterday morning, after I'd lost Madison. I felt more and more sick with every step. We'd already passed the spot on the beach where we'd laid our towels. Now we passed the ice cream stall where Madison had bought our lollies, then the ladies' toilet where I had looked for her.

Shelby stopped as we reached the main square at the heart of the promenade. 'If we talk to Mom we're going to have to explain that we went to the London apartment,' she said anxiously. 'Mom will totally freak when she knows we kept her out of the loop.'

'You're not responsible for your mum,' Jam said with a wry smile. 'If she flips out it's not your fault.'

Shelby looked close to tears and it struck me that having Annie for your mother full time must be hard work. My own mum – my adoptive mum who I grew up with – was always so organised and sensible. Too much so, sometimes. But better that than a mother who was all over the place all the time.

'What really gets me is how Holtwood managed to take Madison without anyone noticing,' Jam said, looking round. 'I mean, the place was more crowded when you were here yesterday and she had to get her all the way up the road to a car or a van. You'd think Madison would have yelled out or screamed or something.'

I stared at the carousel. It was spinning slowly round, still playing 'The Teddy Bear's Picnic'. There was something I wasn't thinking of . . . some small fact, niggling away, just out of reach.

'Maybe Madison did scream and everyone ignored her,' Shelby said darkly.

'Or maybe there was lots of noise,' I said.

The carousel beside us was certainly noisy. Only two children were riding round right now, but both were whooping with delight. 'The Teddy Bear's Picnic' was still blaring out.

'*. . . to the woods today,*
you're in for a big surprise.'

I gasped. Those two notes – on 'surprise' – sounded suddenly familiar.

Another whoop from one of the kids on the carousel.

It all fell into place.

'They're here right now,' I said. 'Holtwood and Madison.'

13

Musical Direction

'What?' Jam stopped walking. 'How can Holtwood and Madison be here? What are you talking about?'

My pulse raced. 'When Holtwood turned off the filter so I could hear Madison speak, I also got a blast of background noise. I heard that carousel music. Just a couple of notes, but I'm sure it was that same tune.'

'You mean they're somewhere near the carousel? *Here?*' Jam looked round.

'But what if Holtwood sees us?' Shelby shrieked. 'She'll know you lied to her. She'll know we're here. Not in London.'

'Behind here.' Jam grabbed our wrists and dragged us behind the carousel booth.

My heart thumped against my ribs. Had I just blown it *again*?

'Oh *no*,' Shelby said. 'She's watching us now.'

'No.' Jam took a step back from the booth. He shook his head. 'No, that doesn't make sense. Holtwood has no idea we're here. There are lots of people around. Even if she was out in plain view she might not see us.'

'And she *isn't* in plain view,' I said. 'She can't be, she's got Madison with her, remember? She'll be hiding somewhere.'

Shelby nodded.

I peered around the carousel booth, trying to take stock. We were in the central square, the beach behind us. To our left was the carousel and the path leading back to the Boondog Shack, the ice cream stalls and the restaurant where we'd met Matt.

To our right was a small row of shops. They stood with their backs to the promenade rail. People were bustling in and out of all of them.

Opposite us was a larger store selling all sorts of beach goods, from sunglasses to inflatable beach toys. It was even busier than the shops on our right. A row of beach huts led away from it.

'How far away from the carousel would you have to be, so that the music still sounded over the phone?' I asked.

'You'd have to be close,' Jam said.

'You're right,' I said. 'We couldn't hear it outside the restaurant, earlier.'

Shelby moved nearer, peering round the carousel booth beside me. 'Maybe she was standing outside one of the shops,' she suggested.

'But Madison was with her,' I said. 'They must have been *inside*.'

Shelby gazed around. 'But all the shops are really busy.'

'We have to check out the whole area,' I said. 'Shelby, you look around the square. Jam, why don't you see if there's any sign of Holtwood or Madison in the shops on the right. I'll look opposite.'

We split up. My palms were sweating as I ran over to the big shop opposite the carousel. One look inside confirmed that there was no way Holtwood could have made her call from its crowded aisles. There were no other shops on this side of the square. No proper buildings at all . . . just the terrace of brightly coloured beach huts stretching along the promenade.

I rubbed my sweaty palms down the front of my jeans and set off along the row. Identical in size and shape – they were all about three or four metres square – the beach huts varied only in the colours chosen to decorate the fronts. Some were painted in bright, strong blues and reds, others in soft pastels. All of them looked well cared for. A few were occupied, with elderly couples sitting out in plastic chairs on the tiny porches.

I sped along. Towards the end of the row of huts, the noise of the carousel music began to fade. Another few metres and it wouldn't be audible at all, which meant there was no way I'd have heard it through Holtwood's phone if she'd been standing here.

The last hut seemed different from the rest. A strip of green paint was peeling off the wooden door. I looked more closely. The wooden boards along the front of the hut – some of which were nailed over the windows – were warped and worn. It looked deserted and uncared for, completely unlike the others in the row. The carousel music was quieter from here, but still clearly audible.

I was about to turn away when I saw it. A tiny doll's shoe. It lay on its side, half covered with dust and sand. I picked it up and my heart lurched into my mouth. This was surely

Tammy's shoe – from the pocket doll Madison had been playing with when she was taken.

Hands shaking, I tried the hut door. It was locked. The brass lock glinted in the sun. Unlike the rest of the hut, it looked smart and expensive. I took out my phone. Seconds later Shelby and Jam appeared, running towards me.

Jam arrived first. He skidded to a halt beside me, then gazed doubtfully from the doll's shoe to the back of the beach hut.

'Do you really think Madison could be in here?' he whispered. 'I can't believe Holtwood and Frank would dare to keep her so close to the beach.'

'I know, but we have to check.' I pointed to the thin wooden slats that made up the beach hut wall. 'Sound could travel through that.'

I leaned against the wood. It was warm against my cheek. No noises came from inside. 'I can't hear anything,' I whispered.

I turned round as Shelby ran up. I showed her the doll's shoe.

'What are you going to do, Lauren?' she whispered.

'Find a way in,' I said.

I ran my palm along the weather-beaten wooden boards. I pressed each one as I passed by, but none of them were loose.

'That lock looks brand new,' Shelby whispered.

'I know,' I said. 'Which is weird on such a shabby old hut.'

Jam examined the door carefully. 'The lock might be new, but the wood around it is rotten,' he said.

I followed his gaze across the promenade. No-one was watching us. We looked at each other. Jam raised his eyebrows.

103

I checked my watch. We had ten minutes until Holtwood called again. And nothing to offer her.

This was our best option for finding Madison.

'Let's do it,' I said.

'Do what?' Shelby squeaked.

'Oh, man,' Jam breathed. He braced himself.

I stood beside him. 'On three,' I said. 'One.'

'You can't break the door down,' Shelby hissed.

'Yes, we can,' I said firmly. 'Two.'

'But—'

'Three.' Together, Jam and I aimed our kicks squarely at the door. It flew open, revealing an apparently empty hut. I glanced quickly round. No-one had seen us.

'Oh, Lauren, you *can't* go in there.' Shelby hopped from foot to foot, clearly hugely agitated.

For a second I felt irritated with her anxiety. Then I thought about the bombshell news hidden in the letter we'd found earlier. I knew Jam was looking at me. My face burned with guilt.

'We have to. There might be more clues to where Madison is,' I said.

'But—'

'Wait here, then, Shelby,' I said, and I led the way into the hut.

14

The Hut

I could see immediately that there was nothing and no-one inside. The hut was totally empty.

Jam followed me in. 'We must have been wrong,' he whispered. 'There's no sign that anyone's been here.'

'And, by the way, you're now breaking into someone else's property,' Shelby added, peering through the open door. 'We shouldn't be here.'

'Wanna call the police again, Shelbs?' I hissed.

She scowled at me, her face all shadowy and spooky-looking in the dim light.

I looked round. I was sure we were close to Madison now, but Jam was right. There was absolutely no sign that anyone else had ever been here. Treading carefully, I edged round the room, peering into the dusty corners. In the distance, the carousel music rose above the shrieks of excited children. It felt like it belonged to a different world.

'There's nothing here, Lauren,' Shelby whispered. 'We need to go.'

'Wait.' Jam's voice echoed across the hut. He was standing in the far corner, peering down at something. 'Look at this.'

I scurried over. A scrap of blue cloth was caught between

two of the floorboards. It looked like it had been torn off a larger garment.

'That's Madison's,' I gasped. 'It's from the top she was wearing when they took her.' I examined the ground. 'Look at the floorboards. There're gaps between the planks here.'

Jam sank to his knees and ran the tips of his fingers around the side of one of the boards.

'There won't be anything underneath,' Shelby insisted. 'Beach huts don't have cellars or—'

'Help me, Lauren,' Jam said.

I squatted beside him and inched my fingers around the opposite side of the board.

'Ready?' he whispered.

I nodded.

'Pull.'

With a creak, the floorboard came away from the floor. Shelby gasped. Jam reached for the next board. I leaned over, helping him move it out of the way.

Beneath us a man-sized hole in the earth below was clearly visible. A rope ladder hung from a metal bar at the top. I peered into the hole. The rope ladder vanished into shadows.

'Do you have a torch?' I whispered.

'Funnily enough, what with it being the middle of the day I didn't think we'd be needing one,' Jam hissed back. He prodded the side of my jeans. 'Use your phone.'

Hands shaking, I shone my phone into the hole. I could just make out the concrete floor of the room below, a couple of metres down.

Jam leaned closer to the hole, peering down into the darkness, then straightened up again.

'I can't hear or see anything,' he said quietly.

'D'you think this is an old smuggler's cave, like the one Mom was trying to take us to the other day?' Shelby whispered.

'Not with all that concrete,' Jam said softly. 'It's not a natural cave . . . it's more likely part of an old mine or an air raid shelter.'

I checked the time. 'Holtwood will be calling soon,' I whispered. 'This is a chance to find Madison before she realises we don't have anything apart from the money to give her.'

'But we don't know for sure if Madison's down there,' Shelby protested.

Jam frowned. 'She's right, Lauren. Maybe we should—'

'We *have* to take a look,' I insisted. 'If Mo's down here we can go back and get help.'

'No way,' Shelby said. 'We should just tell Mom and Rick like we said. They'll know what to do.'

'Will they?' I met Shelby's gaze. 'Even if they do there's no time. We have to look down there before Holtwood rings me again.'

'Well, *I'm* not going.' Shelby backed away. 'I'm gonna call Mom, tell her what's going on.'

'Fine,' I whispered. I sat down at the edge of the hole and eased my legs through.

'Wait, Lauren.' Jam held out the backpack containing the money. 'Here, Shelbs, you can look after that.'

I found the rope ladder with my feet, letting it take my weight. Jam was just giving Shelby something to do so she didn't feel bad about being scared. Personally I didn't much care about her feelings. Let's face it . . . when had she ever cared about mine?

I climbed down the rope ladder. Keeping it steady was tricky, but it got easier as I neared the bottom of the hole. I reached the ground and stepped softly onto the concrete floor. Using my phone as a light, I could see I was standing in an empty room about the same size as the beach hut above. A dug-out tunnel led off on one side.

Shrieks from small children sounded outside, as the carousel music floated towards us.

'If you go down to the woods today . . .'

The hairs on the back of my neck stood up, as Jam slid silently down the rope ladder after me. 'I thought you said this was a bad idea?' I hissed.

'It is.' Jam landed beside me with a soft thud. 'But I can't let you do it on your own.'

'I'm fine,' I muttered.

But Jam wasn't listening. 'This must have been the room Holtwood called you from,' he whispered.

I looked round. There were definitely signs that people had been here: burger wrappers and drink cans were scattered across the floor and a length of rope was loosely coiled in one corner. I tiptoed across the room to the tunnel opposite. It was low-ceilinged with rough, concrete walls and led away from us into pitch black. I stood, listening, at the entrance. Apart

108

from the noises that filtered through from outside, the whole place was eerily silent.

'Let's try through here,' I whispered.

We walked along a few metres. As we rounded a corner, a dim glow appeared in the distance, casting shadows across the concrete.

There. That had to be Holtwood and Madison. With trembling fingers, I pointed towards the light. Jam nodded to show he'd seen it too.

Silently we crept on.

Another few metres, and my phone vibrated in my pocket.

No. It was Sonia Holtwood calling. Had twenty minutes passed already?

Jam clutched my arm, horrified. I hesitated a second.

'I have to bluff her,' I whispered. 'Buy some time.'

'No—' Jam started.

But I'd already brought the phone to my mouth. I shrank back against the cold, concrete wall, trying hard to minimise the sound of my voice as I spoke. The dim light we were following was still a long way in the distance, but I couldn't tell how well sound would travel along the tunnel.

'Hello?' I whispered.

'Did you find the things Sam hid?' the filtered voice snarled.

'Yes,' I lied.

'What was there?'

I thought of my grandmother – Sam's mum. I'd always got on well with her and my Gramps. They were both living in a nursing home now in the States. Life there seemed a million miles away.

'A diamond necklace and matching earrings,' I lied. 'For me and Shelby. They . . . they belonged to Sam's mother. She wants us to have them. And they're worth, like, over a million dollars.'

Jam shook my arm, his hand open in a gesture of dismay.

Why are you telling her that? he mouthed.

I turned away.

'Right.' A pause on the other end of the line. 'You've got two hours to get back here. I'll text the place for the next exchange.'

She rang off.

'What the hell, Lauren?' Jam hissed.

I pointed in the direction of the glimmering light. 'We just needed a bit of time,' I whispered. 'We've got two more hours.'

'Then let's go back and get help,' Jam whispered.

'But Holtwood and Madison are right here.' I started walking, but Jam grabbed my arm and pulled me back.

'Wait,' he hissed into my ear. 'I came down here with you because Holtwood hadn't called yet and there was a bit of time to see if Madison was down here, without doing anything stupid – but now you've made things worse by inventing jewellery that doesn't even exist and—'

'I *had* to.'

'If we go any further Holtwood will see us,' Jam said. 'That guy, Frank, is probably here too, and—'

110

'It's a chance to rescue Mo.'

'Rescue her?' Jam hissed. 'From people with guns? Anyway, what are you going to say when Holtwood realises you don't have any diamonds?'

'Go back then.' I crept off, my heart pounding. Couldn't Jam see we *had* to find Madison? This might be her last chance.

I could feel Jam still behind me, but I didn't look round. We rounded another curve in the tunnel. Now the low mumble of voices drifted towards us. I squinted into the gloom as the source of both the light and the voices became clear. A dim glow was shining out through a door, halfway along the tunnel ahead.

Trembling, I tiptoed closer.

Closer.

Sweat beaded on my forehead. The back of my neck prickled as we reached the door.

Low voices drifted towards us again. The door was open a fraction. A man and a woman were talking inside, but so quietly I couldn't make out what they were saying or even if they were, as I suspected, Frank and Sonia.

Footsteps sounded inside the room. Jam and I exchanged a terrified look. They were coming towards the door.

We sprang back, against the wall behind the door. It opened, slamming back against us. Jam caught the handle, holding it steady so it didn't fly shut again.

More footsteps.

'Come on.' That was definitely Frank.

I heard a sniff and a stumble. I peered round the edge of the door. Frank had Madison by the arm. He hauled her along the tunnel away from us . . . in the opposite direction from the room that led up to the beach hut.

Madison was bound at the wrists with rope. Strips of cloth had been wound round her eyes and her mouth.

Anger like I'd never known filled me. How could anyone do that to a little girl? It was inhuman.

Jam yanked me back, behind the cover of the door, as a woman appeared. I froze, my anger transforming into terror. Was that Sonia Holtwood? I could only see her from behind and she was wearing a long jacket that concealed her body shape, but it had to be her.

Out of nowhere my legs started shaking. Panic gripped me. I couldn't move. Everything that had happened to me nearly two years ago flooded back. Being left for dead in the freezing wood . . . nearly drowning on that boat . . .

'We can't help Madison like this.' Jam was shaking my arm, hissing in my ear. 'We should go back.'

'No.' I couldn't leave my baby sister. I *couldn't.*

I darted out from Jam's hold, creeping after Holtwood along the tunnel. She disappeared into the shadows ahead.

Jam caught up with me. He grabbed my arm again. 'Come *on,*' he whispered.

I wrenched my arm away and with that sudden movement, my mobile clattered to the floor.

'What was that?' Frank's voice echoed out of the shadows along the tunnel ahead.

A second later footsteps sounded, heading towards us.

Oh no. I froze. Jam snatched up my phone, shoved it into my hands. We turned and tore back along the tunnel towards the room below the beach hut.

I glanced over my shoulder. Frank was chasing after us.

'Hey!' His shout echoed off the concrete.

Jam sped up. I ran faster too, my breath now coming in gasps. On we ran. Through the tunnel. Into the room where the rope ladder still dangled in the corner.

Shouts echoed behind us.

'Stop!' Frank yelled.

Jam grabbed the rope ladder, holding it steady. 'Climb!' he ordered.

There was no time to argue with him, to make him go first. I scrambled up, up. I reached the hole in the beach hut above. I hauled myself through. Jam was climbing up behind me. Frank skidded to a halt at his feet. Grabbed Jam's leg.

'Come on,' I urged.

Jam kicked Frank away. Climbed up another step.

Come on. Come on.

Jam was almost at the top of the rope ladder. I reached out my hand to help him out. But Frank grabbed his leg and yanked him down to the floor.

No.

I froze, unable to reach Jam. He was clinging to the bottom of the ladder. Frank was trying to pull him off.

And then the woman came running over. She stood beside them, her gaze fixed on Jam's face.

She wasn't Sonia Holtwood. She was much younger with a narrower, longer face.

The good news was that she hadn't seen me.

The bad news was that she had Frank's gun and was pointing it at Jam.

15

Help

Jam looked up at me. *Go*, he mouthed silently.

'Get him off the ladder!' the woman who was not Sonia Holtwood screamed. 'Get after the girl.'

I backed away from the hole, then turned and raced out of the beach hut. Shelby came running up, backpack flapping on her back. 'I didn't call Mom yet. What happ—'

'Run!' I gasped at her.

She stood, gawping at me. 'Where's Jam?' She frowned. 'Where's Madison?'

I shoved her in the shoulder. 'Come on!' I urged again. 'Go!'

I tore past the row of beach huts, not bothering to check if she was following me. The noise and bustle of the prom-enade filled the air. I raced to the square, past the carousel, still playing 'The Teddy Bear's Picnic', and on up the street, away from the sea.

Shelby caught up with me and we ran on. After a few minutes, we reached the holiday home. We stopped just outside the front garden, both of us gasping . . . trying to get our breath back.

I looked back down the road. There was no sign of anyone following us.

What did that mean? Had we lost them? Or had the kidnappers given up the chase?

'What the hell happened?' Shelby panted. 'Where's Jam?'

I stood shaking in the sunlight as the full reality of the situation sank in.

They had Jam . . . Frank and this woman. I had no idea who she was. I had no idea about anything. All I knew was that in trying to save Madison I'd only managed to lose Jam as well.

I glanced over at the holiday home. Annie was inside, walking past the living-room window. She was speaking to someone – Rick presumably – twisting her hands together.

What on earth was I going to say to her? In that instant it hit me how stupid and selfish I had been earlier. I hadn't thought through what Jam and I would do down in the tunnel, even though I knew we were up against two ruthless adults with a gun. I'd been so obsessed with finding Madison – and so convinced I was dealing with Sonia Holtwood – that I thought I'd be able to handle whatever situation I came up against.

Instead of which I'd only made mistakes. I'd lied to the female kidnapper, promising her diamond jewellery I didn't have on top of the two million pounds cash. And I'd lost Jam. A terrible raw pain swelled inside me. Whether or not he was helping because he wanted to or because he felt he should, Jam had been with me every step of the way. He had warned me we didn't have a plan for rescuing Madison and now *he* was the one who was paying the price for it.

I fingered the wooden oval round my neck. *Please be OK, Jam. Please.*

116

Beside me, Shelby swore. 'Will you *talk* to me, Lauren?' she said. 'Where's Jam? Did you find Madison? What happened?'

I gritted my teeth. The last thing I wanted to do was explain what had gone on under that beach hut.

'We saw Madison . . .' I hesitated, hating having to say the words out loud. 'But they stopped us. They . . . they caught Jam.'

Shelby blinked, shocked. 'Sonia Holtwood has Jam now?' she said. 'As well as Madison?'

'She's *not* Sonia Holtwood,' I said savagely, realising as I spoke that this meant I knew less than ever about who we were dealing with – and what they were capable of. 'The man is Frank – Holtwood used him two years ago. But the woman is someone else altogether. Not Sonia Holtwood.'

'What do you mean?' Shelby's face expressed confusion.

For goodness' sake. All my frustration and anxiety seemed to roll into a ball at the sight of her blank incomprehension. I took a deep breath then I hurled everything I felt into Shelby's face.

'I wish it was y—' I stopped and dug my fingers into my palms to stop myself saying it . . .

'What?' Shelby's frown deepened. 'Wish *what*?'

'Nothing.' I couldn't say it. I didn't mean it. It was too cruel.

Shelby drew in her breath. 'You were going to say you wished it was *me*. That you wished the kidnappers had taken me instead of Madison and Jam?'

'No, of course not.' But I couldn't meet Shelby's gaze.

She took a step away from me. I looked up. Hurt flashed through her eyes and for a moment, I thought she was going to burst into tears or hit me or scream. But she didn't do any of those things. She just stared at me for a few seconds as her expression hardened, like a mask.

Guilt spread through me like a poison.

'I'm sorry, Shelb—'

'Don't.' Shelby held up her hand, cutting me off. Her voice was hard and cold. 'So what do we do now?'

I bit my lip. 'Well, we have less than two hours before the next exchange. The kidnappers think we're bringing them a diamond necklace and earrings that don't exist so unless we rob a jewellery store in the next ninety minutes, we're basically screwed.'

Shelby stared at me. She said nothing.

I swallowed, shuffling from foot to foot. I knew she was thinking about how she had wanted to involve the police in the first place. *Jeez*, it hit me like a thunderbolt. She'd been totally right. I mean, OK, so involving the cops put Madison at risk.

But Madison was at terrible risk already.

Shelby glanced over towards the holiday home. I followed her gaze to the brightly painted blue gate and the front garden, overgrown with flowers. Annie was still visible through the window, her back to the pavement where we were standing.

I took a deep breath. 'I think we should tell Annie and Rick everything,' I said. 'I think we should tell them it's time to call the police and tell *them* everything.' I wanted to add: *like you said we should*. But the words somehow stuck in my throat.

118

Shelby gave a curt nod. 'Right.'

And together we walked up the road to the house.

'But what are we going to do if the police mess up?' Annie wailed for the fifth time. 'I can just imagine them going in heavy and . . . and my baby getting hurt . . .' She dissolved into tears again.

We were in the kitchen of the holiday home. Annie was pacing in front of the door to the garden. Shelby was sitting at the table. Like me, she was watching Annie but saying nothing.

I don't think she knew what to say to calm Annie down.

I certainly didn't.

I'd imagined – more a hope than a reasoned thought – that once we'd told Annie everything she would pull herself together and, at the very least, agree that we need to phone the police and hand over responsibility for rescuing Madison to the authorities.

But Annie, once again, had fallen into a panicky mess of terror and indecision.

I'd briefly wondered if she would question me more closely about my search for valuables in the London flat. But she'd just looked amazed that Jam and I had thought we'd find anything there. She didn't seem at all concerned that I might have stumbled across Sam's letters. I was more sure than ever that she didn't know about them.

This made it easier not to deal with the discovery myself. Shelby's letter was in Jam's pocket, of course, but I'd shoved mine away in my bedroom. I still felt numb about Sam not being my biological dad, like the whole thing wasn't real.

Madison and Jam being taken, on the other hand, was urgent and overwhelming.

I glanced over at Rick. He was gazing thoughtfully at Annie. He exuded calm. The only indication that he was in any way stressed was the way his little finger tapped against the counter.

Surely he would know what to do about the kidnappers?

'Rick?' I said. 'What do you think?'

He glanced from Annie to me. 'It's going to be all right,' he said firmly.

'You don't know that, Rick, honey.' Annie wrung her hands together.

'Mom, please.' Shelby sounded close to tears.

'Yes, Annie,' Rick repeated slowly. 'I do know. We're going to make this work.'

The three of us stared at him.

'What do you think we should do?' I asked.

'What you and Shelby have already suggested,' Rick said. 'I think we should contact the police.'

'But—' Annie started.

'I'm not saying we dial 999,' Rick interrupted. 'We need the exchange to go ahead so we can get Madison and Jam back as fast as possible.' He looked down at his watch. 'That only gives us just over an hour and a half. Not enough time for a proper police response to the situation. But I've got a mate who's a cop . . . his name's Cooper Trent. He used to work on kidnap and ransom cases. I should have thought of him earlier. He'll help. I know he will. If he's there for back-up then we'll be able to handle whatever this couple who've got Jam and Madison do.'

I felt my shoulders release as he spoke. Looking at Annie and Shelby, it was clear they felt the same. Relief was etched on both their faces.

'Are you sure, honey?' Annie said with a sniff.

'Absolutely.' Rick gave her a warm smile. 'Cooper's the man. If he and I can block the kidnappers off there's no way they can run off like they did last time.'

I frowned. 'But how can just two of you block them off? Suppose they pick a place for the exchange with lots of exits.'

'They're not picking the place for the exchange,' Rick said. His voice was stern and completely authoritative.

I gaped at him.

'We're telling *them* where the exchange will take place,' he went on. 'And by "we" I mean "I".' He paused. 'I should never have let you take their calls, Lauren. I should have stepped up sooner. But I'm doing it now. When your phone rings, *I'm* answering. Let them deal with someone their own size.'

I stared at him, impressed.

Annie flew round the table and hurled herself into his arms. 'Oh, Rick, thank you, thank you,' she sobbed.

I looked at Shelby, hoping we could share a moment of acknowledgement. Annie might be a flake, but Rick was pretty cool.

But Shelby didn't meet my gaze. Her expression was unreadable.

16

The Exchange

Half an hour later and it was all sorted. Rick had spoken to his friend, the ex-cop, Cooper Trent, and arranged to meet him on the way to the exchange. Shortly afterwards, the kidnappers rang and Rick took the call.

He was amazing. Completely unflappable and holding firm to everything he'd said earlier.

'Well, I'm talking to you now,' he said into the phone. 'There weren't any diamonds. Lauren just made that up because she was scared.'

I could feel my face flushing. Though what Rick said was true, I didn't much like hearing it.

'If you want your money you'd better listen to me,' Rick went on. 'We'll meet at Chantler's Cross in thirty minutes. Leave your van by the stile down the track. Bring the kids into the field. We'll do the exchange there. You get the cash. We get the kids. Deal?'

Annie gripped my arm as we listened.

'D'you know where that is, Mom?' Shelby whispered on her other side.

'Yes, we drove past it when we had that picnic on Sandcove beach last week,' Annie said.

I nodded. I didn't remember Chantler's Cross, but I remembered Annie's crazy picnic. She'd brought soft rolls (no butter) and a bag of carrots, so I'd made carrot-stick sandwiches for me and Madison. I'd munched away while Madison whispered in my ear a long story about her pocket dolls Tammy and Tilda. It was all made up, just Madison's imagination firing away like it always did, but she'd spoken about the dolls so passionately it was as if they were real people.

Rick came off the phone to the kidnappers.

'Did they mind it wasn't me doing the exchange?' I asked.

Rick made a face. 'They still want you there with the money. As you heard, I told them those diamonds you've promised them don't exist.'

'Were they really OK about that?' I asked.

Rick shrugged. 'No, but there isn't anything they can do, is there?'

I frowned. Would the kidnappers really let it go?

'Don't worry about it, Lauren,' Rick said firmly. 'You and I need to go to the field now. We'll hook up with Cooper on the way. Just keep a tight hold of that two million.'

I squirmed in my seat, realising I had something else to admit to now. 'Er . . . it took about sixty pounds to pay for our train tickets earlier.'

'You mean the money's light?' Rick said. 'Annie, how much cash do you have on you?'

'Oh my goodness.' Annie's hands fluttered nervously over her purse. 'There should be enough . . . I brought lots of British money with me . . .'

'It'll be fine,' Rick said firmly.

And it was. Shelby and I checked the money in the backpack and added exactly the right amount we needed from Annie's purse. As we worked methodically at the table, Annie herself paced around the kitchen. Tears were streaming down her face.

'I should come with you,' she wept. 'I want to be there when we get Madison.'

Rick eyed her. I could tell that, like me, he thought Annie's presence during the exchange was an extremely bad idea, and felt a surge of pride that he had no such doubts about me.

'Maybe it would be better for Madison if you stayed at home, sweetheart,' Rick said. 'I mean, it's going to be pretty tense out there and the kidnappers won't be expecting you, and if you stay here you can have the house all ready for the little one to come back to.'

'Do you really think so?' Annie sobbed.

'Yes,' Rick said. He looked at me and Shelby. 'Agreed, girls?'

I nodded.

'Rick's right on this, Mom,' Shelby said. 'You stay here.'

'OK,' Annie sniffed.

'And *I'll* go with Rick and Lauren,' Shelby said.

What?

'I don't know that's such a great idea,' I said.

'That's so typical of you, Lauren,' Shelby said bitterly. 'Why should *I* be left behind?'

'You're not part of the deal,' I insisted.

'The kidnappers sent me to the London apartment, same as you,' Shelby retorted.

I rolled my eyes. Why did Shelby have to make everything such a competition?

Rick sighed. 'OK, that's settled then. Annie stays here to make sure everything's ready for Madison's return. Shelby and Lauren drive to the exchange site with me. We'll pick up Cooper on the way.'

Cooper was leaning against a hedge, waiting, as we swung into the lay-by. He looked like a maverick cop from a TV series – tall and well-built, with a shock of straw-coloured hair swept off his face. He was in his thirties, or early forties, I guessed, like Rick. However, he seemed far more macho than Rick, walking with a definite hint of swagger.

We got out of the car and Rick introduced me and Shelby. Cooper said 'hello' very seriously, then walked round the outside of the car and checked the tyres.

'Just making sure we're good for a getaway,' he said.

A moment later we set off again. Chantler's Cross was about three miles away. The 'cross' itself was just an ancient stone marker set along a country road surrounded by fields. We took the turning immediately after the cross, a narrow dirt track in the middle of a wooded area. We parked halfway down the track, just before a stile, then climbed over the stile into a large field surrounded on all sides by trees. Most of the field wasn't visible from the dirt track, let alone the road beyond. A perfect, private location for the exchange.

I followed Rick and Cooper across the field. The earth under the sparse browned grass was hard and dry. The two men talked in low voices. I looked around, feeling nervous, the bag containing the money bumping against my legs. It was 8.15. The kidnappers would be here soon.

What if they didn't bring Madison or Jam?

What if they got angry that I'd lied about the diamond jewellery?

What if they killed us all?

We reached the centre of the field and waited. Rick and Cooper chatted in low voices. Shelby and I didn't speak to each other at all.

The minutes ticked past. I switched off my phone. I didn't want to risk it ringing in the middle of the exchange, and after not getting hold of me all day, Mum was bound to call again soon.

It was 8.30 now and the moon shone through the dusk, highlighting the silhouettes of the trees that waved in the twilight sky. I could hear nothing, apart from the occasional swish of distant traffic. Annie phoned Rick. I couldn't hear what she was saying but, from Rick's soothing tone, I gathered that she was still in tears.

Rick came off his mobile with a sigh. I set the backpack down at my feet. The kidnappers still weren't here and it was almost twenty minutes after the time we'd agreed for the exchange.

'What the hell's keeping them?' Cooper muttered.

Rick shrugged.

'I'm going to take a look over that stile down the track,' I said. 'See if there's any sign of them.'

'Not on your own, you're not.' Rick accompanied me to the stile. Shelby – clearly not wanting to be left out – came too. We peered over the bars. Rick's car was parked up on the left, a dark shadow at the side of the dirt track. I peered in the other direction. There, in the distance, two small headlamps were coming towards us.

'That's got to be them,' I said.

'Oh my goodness.' Shelby's hands fluttered to her chest in a gesture I recognised from Annie.

'Come on.' Rick led us back to the middle of the field, where Cooper waited. The sound of an engine drifted towards us across the night air. The kidnappers were getting closer and closer.

'Look.' Cooper pointed towards the dirt track, where the white van from the first exchange attempt was pulling up beside the stile. The lights switched off, but I could still make out Frank's outline as he got out of the driving seat and walked to the back of the van.

A moment later Frank had bundled Jam and Madison – both blindfolded and with their hands tied behind them – over the stile. My heart raced at the sight of them. They looked so vulnerable. This *had* to work. Frank marched them towards us across the field. The woman I'd mistaken for Sonia Holtwood strode behind them, her hair tied back in a ponytail. Frank's gun glinted in her hand.

I shivered, realising how easily she'd fooled me.

127

'Here we go,' Cooper said softly.

Frank and the woman stopped about fifty metres away. Jam and Madison stood beside them. I could see Jam speaking, but was too far away to hear what he said.

'Bring the money over!' the woman shouted. She was definitely American.

'Send the kids first!' Rick yelled.

The woman turned to Frank. A moment later he was untying the blindfolds round Madison and Jam's eyes. As soon as she saw me, Madison started to run. Frank grabbed her arm. He said something to her. Again, I was too far away to hear. Madison hung her head.

'Jam and Madison will walk towards you, Lauren,' the woman ordered, 'while you walk towards us with the money.'

Jam reached for Madison's hand as they made their way slowly across the field. Madison stumbled on the grass. Jam squeezed her hand tighter, but kept his eyes fixed on me.

Rick prodded me in the back. 'Go on, Lauren,' he said firmly. 'Start walking. It's going to be OK.'

I picked up the backpack full of money and moved forward. My legs were trembling slightly and I had another flashback to the earlier exchange attempt. Somehow this one felt spookier – what with the field and the darkness – and yet safer too. Whatever happened, I knew that Rick and Cooper were right behind me.

I drew closer to Jam and Madison. They were both looking at me intently. As soon as we got near enough to talk without the others hearing, I spoke.

'Are you OK?' I asked.

'We're fine,' Jam said.

'Lauren, I'm scared.' Madison's voice was smaller than I could ever remember it.

'Don't be scared, sweetheart,' I said. 'Mommy's waiting for you at home. It's almost over.'

We reached each other. Stopped.

'Keep coming!' Frank ordered.

'See you in a minute,' Jam said.

I walked on, past them, towards Frank and the woman. The backpack strap felt sweaty in my hand. I was twenty metres away. Ten. Getting closer.

'Stop there!' Rick called out behind me. 'Lauren's come far enough!' he yelled to the kidnappers.

I stopped and glanced over my shoulder. Jam and Madison had reached the place where Cooper, Rick and Shelby were waiting. Rick had picked Madison up in his arms. She was clinging to him like a monkey, her face buried in his neck.

'OK!' Rick yelled. 'Lauren's going to put down the money and walk away. My colleague is going to take the other kids to the car. You've got what you wanted. We're done.'

I put down the backpack and took a step back.

'Wait.' The woman pointed her gun at me. 'Stay there while I check the money.'

I stopped. The woman ran forward and grabbed the bag, then raced back to Frank.

I stood still. The field was completely silent as the woman opened the backpack and reached in her hand. A breeze ruffled my hair, cool against the sweat on my forehead.

129

I glanced sideways. Out of the corner of my eye I could see Cooper and Shelby helping Jam and Madison over the stile. Their hands were still tied, but I knew Rick had a penknife in his car we could use to cut the rope.

'What is this?' The woman's shrill voice filled the air. 'Lauren?'

I spun round to face her. What was happening now?

'Where's the money?' The woman levelled her gun directly at me.

It took me a moment to register what she was saying. And then I looked down. The grass at the woman's feet was littered with newspaper. Most of it was in bundles, clearly resembling the shape and size of the notes we had put in the backpack earlier. A few pieces had come loose and fluttered across the grass, the newsprint highlighted in the moonlight.

I looked up from the bundles of newspaper to the backpack that dangled from the woman's hand.

And the terrible truth hit me like a fist.

The money was gone.

17

The Choice

I stared, stupidly, at the empty backpack, my brain taking a few seconds to catch up with my eyes.

Where was the money?

Rick ran towards me. His eyes were wide open. Completely shocked. Clearly he had no more idea what was happening than I did.

The woman pointed her gun at him.

'Stop!' she demanded. 'What's going on?'

'I don't know,' Rick stammered. 'The money was in there. Someone's switched the real notes with those bits of newspaper.'

'Give me that.' Frank tore the gun out of the woman's hand and raced across the field to where Cooper had disappeared with Shelby, Jam and Madison.

Oh no, oh no, oh no.

'I promise you, we thought the money was—' I started.

'Shut UP!' The woman advanced towards me. 'This is your fault, you little witch!'

Spit flew from her mouth. Her eyes were wild with fury. I backed away.

'Stand still,' she ordered, raising her fist.

I turned and ran, my heart thumping against my ribs. If I could just reach the trees at the edge of the field . . . The woman pounded after me, her feet thudding across the dry earth.

'No!' Rick shouted.

I prayed he was running after me, trying to catch the woman and stop her. But I didn't dare look round. Her footsteps sounded close. I reached the trees. Tore through them. Leaves and twigs cracked underfoot. I sped past a bush, desperate for somewhere to hide. It was almost dark, but there was still enough light to see by. If I could just make it into the next field . . .

I darted left, then right, past more trees. I was in the thick of the wood now, with no idea which direction anything was in. I stopped for a second. I could hear footsteps nearby, but it was impossible to work out exactly where they were coming from.

I looked round, desperate. A sheet of corrugated iron lay propped against a fallen tree trunk. I rushed over and crawled underneath it. I had to curl into a tight ball to fit. I lay motionless, the side of my face pressed into the dry earth.

Footsteps were still crashing around nearby. I kept as still as possible. My left leg was cramped from being tucked up underneath me, but I didn't dare move.

And then, at last, Rick's call echoed through the night air.

'Lauren?' he said softly, his voice a loud whisper. 'Lauren, are you here?'

I hesitated a second, then pushed the corrugated iron sheet off me. Rick was just a few metres away, standing by a tree. He walked towards me.

'Are you all right?' he said.

I nodded, brushing myself down. 'Where are they?' I whispered.

'The man is still chasing after Cooper and the kids,' Rick said softly. 'I just saw the woman going across the field away from us.' He put his arm round my shoulders and gave my arm a squeeze. 'Come on, we need to get out of here. I spotted a gap in the trees where we can get out onto the track and back to the others.'

We hurried through the wood. It was darker now and the full moon shone high in the sky.

'What happened to the money?' I whispered as we ran.

'I don't know . . .' Rick looked anxious. 'It was right there in the bag when we left the house. And the bag was with us the whole time.'

We ran on. I powered past a clump of fallen branches. Fear filled my chest, tightening every muscle. What would happen to Jam and Madison if Cooper hadn't got them away . . . if Frank caught up with them? They were already gagged and bound – completely defenceless.

We raced into a clearing. 'We have to—'

With a crash, the woman came stumbling through the trees towards us. She saw me. Saw Rick.

For a second I froze. We stared at each other across the clearing.

133

'Stop!' the woman said.

For a second I hesitated. And then I realised that Frank had taken her gun earlier . . . that she had no obvious weapon . . . I spun round.

'Run!' I shrieked. I pelted back into the wood.

I could hear Rick crashing along behind me. I pounded on, my breath burning in my throat.

And then Rick cried out in pain.

I skidded to a halt. Turned. Somehow Rick was no longer right behind me. He cried out again. I spun around, searching the trees. Where was he?

'Lauren, I've got Rick,' the woman called. 'If you don't come back I'll kill him.'

There was a long pause. Surely she was bluffing. I stood, motionless, between two trees. I could hear footsteps drawing nearer. Two sets. The woman's and Rick's.

'There's nowhere you can run anyway,' the woman snarled. 'If you don't come back now I'll kill Rick and we'll catch you anyway.'

I didn't believe that. It was getting darker with every passing minute and I was sure I could find a way back to the road without the kidnappers seeing me. It wouldn't be easy to get away, but I could give it a go.

And yet, how could I leave Rick here to die? He'd tried to help us. I couldn't just abandon him.

'Aaagh!' Rick yelled out in pain again.

I tried to steel myself. Rick didn't matter. Rick wasn't even my family. Goodness knows what had happened to Jam and Madison.

They were the people I cared about.

'AAAGH!' Another agonised scream.

'It's up to you, Lauren.' The woman's voice was ice cold. I had no doubt she meant what she said. 'I'll count to three. Then Rick dies.'

I stood, waiting.

'One.'

What should I do?

'Two.'

I took a deep breath.

'Three.'

'OK!' I shouted. 'I'm coming.'

I walked towards the sound of the woman's voice, back to the clearing. She was standing by a tree. Rick was beside her, clutching the side of his head. It looked like she'd hit him with something.

'Come here, Lauren,' the woman said.

But before I could move, Frank burst into the clearing, a tote bag in his hand. He didn't notice me on the edge of the trees.

'I got the money,' he panted. 'Cooper had it.'

Cooper? But he was Rick's friend . . . an ex-policeman. Why would he have taken the money?

'I knocked him out,' Frank went on. 'I locked him and the kids in your car, Rick.'

Rick froze.

I gasped. Why was Frank talking to Rick as if he knew him?

135

The woman swore. She grabbed the gun from Frank's pocket and levelled it at me. 'Frank, you are a total dumbass.'

'What?' Frank looked round and saw me for the first time. 'Oh,' he said.

Rick still hadn't taken his eyes off me. '*Oh*,' he mimicked. 'Well done, Frank,' he said sarcastically.

'You?' The word escaped out of my mouth as a hoarse breath.

Rick said nothing, but his eyes burned with guilty fury. And I knew the truth at last.

Rick was one of the kidnappers.

18

The Edge

Rick was one of the kidnappers.

How was that even possible?

The woman standing beside him swore loudly. '*Now* what are we going to do?' she shouted.

Rick put his hands on his head. He paced up and down. 'We'll work it out, Julianne,' he said.

I stared at him, dumbstruck. Rick was in league with this woman, Julianne. He had betrayed Annie and me and my sisters.

I couldn't believe it.

Julianne kept her gun trained on me. 'Work it out *how*, Rick?' she demanded, her eyes blazing.

'I need to think,' Rick snapped. He pointed at me. 'Tie her up, Frank.'

'This isn't my fault.' Frank strode towards me, fishing a length of rope out of his pocket.

'Then whose fault is it?' Julianne fumed. 'All that planning and everything screwed up at the eleventh hour.'

'If it wasn't for me there wouldn't have been a plan,' Frank protested. He dragged my hands roughly behind my back. 'I'm the one that told you guys about this family.'

So kidnapping Madison had started with Frank? The rope around my wrists bit into my skin but I barely noticed. My mind was reeling, trying to take in what I was hearing.

'Yeah, well, I wish you hadn't bothered,' Julianne snapped. 'Man, this is such a mess.'

'Will you two shut up for a moment,' Rick demanded. 'Let me think.'

'Don't tell me to shut up,' Julianne shouted. 'This is your fault too, Rick.'

'*My* fault?' Rick turned on her.

'Yes. You brought that animal Cooper into it. You *knew* what he was like after that last con job.'

Con job? So Cooper wasn't a policeman after all, but another criminal. My mind flashed back to what Frank had said a minute ago, when he'd burst into the clearing.

'What about Madison and Jam and Shelby?' I turned to Frank, desperately trying to pull my wrists free of the rope. 'You said you left them locked in the car with Cooper, but—?'

'I only needed to bring Cooper in because you got greedy, Julianne,' Rick shouted over me. 'You sent the girls on a wild goose chase for valuables that didn't exist. They'd have called the real police if I hadn't pretended Cooper was a cop. Man, I can't believe he tried to double-cross us.'

'Please,' I persisted, still struggling against the rope around my wrist. 'What about my—'

'*You saw* the email on Sam Purditt's laptop,' Julianne shouted. 'He *said* there was something in the apartment. "*Something of huge value*" . . . remember? Anyway, two million was never enough. We should have been asking for more in the first place.'

'No way,' Rick snarled. 'And I don't know why you're so angry. It's *my* cover that's been blown.'

'None of this matters now,' Frank insisted. 'Come on, we need to get out of here.'

He grabbed my arm and pulled me after him.

'Please, Frank.' I ran beside him. 'Are Jam and my sisters OK?'

'I told you. They're locked in the car with Cooper. He's out cold for now,' Frank said. 'Now shut up and keep moving.'

A few seconds later we emerged through the trees onto the dirt track. I could see the kidnappers' white van by the stile. I knew that Rick's car, containing Cooper and the others, was parked further up the track.

I opened my mouth to call out, but Julianne pressed her gun against my ribs.

'Don't even think about it,' she hissed.

My heart pounded.

'OK.' Rick cleared his throat. 'Julianne, you stay here with Lauren. Frank, follow me.'

The two men set off up the track.

'Where are they going?' I said.

'Rick's getting the van,' Julianne snapped.

'What about Frank?'

'He's going to deal with Cooper.'

'What does that mean?' I said. 'What about Jam and my sisters?'

139

'If they do what Frank says they won't get hurt. Now stop talking.' She prodded my side with the gun to reinforce her point.

As I watched the two men disappearing into the shadows along the track, I tried to take in everything I'd learned. Rick had involved Cooper to make it look like he'd brought in the police. And then Cooper had tried to double-cross Rick by taking the money from the backpack just before the exchange. I frowned, trying to work out when Cooper could have made the switch. *Jeez*, it must have been when Rick, Shelby and I went to the stile to see if the kidnappers were coming.

With a flush of shame, I remembered how proud I'd been that Rick had wanted me, rather than Annie, along for the exchange.

Once again, I had totally messed up.

'I guess you're not as smart as you thought you were, are you?' Julianne sneered, her words echoing my own thoughts. '*I* fooled you, anyway, pretending to be Sonia Holtwood.'

'Why did you do that?' I asked.

'One of Frank's better ideas, like kidnapping Madison from a beach . . . to convince you I was her . . . that we meant business,' Julianne snapped. 'Get you running along the wrong track.'

My heart sank. The kidnappers' lies had worked. I'd been totally taken in. Worse, thanks to everything I'd done afterwards, I'd got Jam into danger without actually helping Madison at all.

And now I was paying the price. I just had to hope that Jam, Madison and Shelby weren't paying it too.

A minute later, Rick was back with the van.

He jumped down and opened the back doors.

'Get in, Lauren,' he said.

My pulse raced. 'Where are you taking me?'

'No questions,' Rick said. He grabbed my arm and shoved me inside the van.

'How could you do this, Rick?' I said.

He didn't meet my gaze, just slammed the van door shut on me. My stomach twisted into a sick knot. Rick had seemed strong and resourceful. Of all the adults around, he was the one I thought I could best rely on.

And instead he was the worst of the lot.

A few seconds later, we drove off. I slumped down onto the floor of the van, my back pressed against the cold metal.

What were Rick and Julianne going to do with me now?

I don't know how long we drove for, but at last the van stopped. Rick opened the back doors and pulled me out. He shoved a sack over my head, then steered me across the uneven ground.

The wind was stronger here than it had been before and I could smell the sea. Rick kept a strong grip on the rope tied round my wrists. We walked for about a minute. I couldn't see anything through the sack. It was pitch black.

Rick and Julianne muttered to each other as we walked, but I couldn't hear what they were saying. All the hairs on the back of my neck were raised. There was a hollow pit where my guts should be.

'What are you doing?' I said several times. 'Where are you taking me?' But they ignored me.

The ground grew more uneven and sloped downwards. I could feel stones underfoot, their sharp edges cutting against my trainers. At last we stopped walking. The wind was really fierce now. It was pressing the sack flat against my face. The hessian was rough against my skin.

'This is a good place,' Julianne said.

'Yes, it's perfect,' Rick agreed.

He pulled the sack off my head. I gasped. I was standing between Rick and Julianne on a ledge on the side of a cliff. It was a sheer drop down to the jagged rocks eighty metres below. The sea crashed against them, then stretched away, like a black shroud, towards the dark sky beyond.

I glanced around, hoping to see lights nearby . . . some sign of human life. But the place was completely deserted. The waves smashed beneath me, the salt spray licking up at my face. And I realised what Rick and Julianne were going to do.

I was the only person who knew Rick had betrayed us. If I wasn't around he could go back to Annie for another day or two, then simply slide out of her life, with no questions asked.

He and Julianne would have the two million pounds. They would pay Frank off.

And, before all that, I would fall to my death into the sea below.

19

No Way Out

I stepped back, pressing my heels against the cold rock behind me. The ledge we were all standing on was less than a metre deep.

Rick checked his watch.

'We rendezvous with Frank in twenty minutes,' he said.

Julianne set down the tote bag containing the two million pounds on the ledge beside her.

'Let's do it,' she said.

'No,' I said desperately. 'Please, Rick. I won't tell Annie about you. You can keep the money.'

'Shut up,' Julianne snapped. 'Come on, Rick.'

'Wait a second, we don't want Lauren found with this rope on,' Rick said.

I felt the cold sharp metal of a knife against my skin. I shrank away, but strong hands grabbed my wrists.

'Hold still,' Rick ordered. He sliced the knife through the rope.

My hands were free.

'You can't do this,' I insisted. 'If you do this, Annie will work out it was you.'

'No she won't,' Rick said. 'I'll see her later. Explain I need a bit of space after the whole thing with Madison.'

143

'You still won't get away with it,' I insisted. My heart was pumping like it would explode. 'Rick, how can you *do* this? *Any* of this?'

'It was supposed to be just the money,' Rick said defiantly. 'When we started I was just going to go after the money in the accounts, but that didn't work, so we had to take the little one.'

'Ready, Rick?' Julianne sounded tense. The wind was whipping through her hair and flapping at her jacket.

As Rick put the knife down, Julianne gripped my arm just above the elbow. I stared at her fingers, curled round my jumper, an idea forming.

This was it.

With a sudden, deliberate, movement, I pulled away from Julianne. She tightened her grip on my arm, trying to yank me back to her. But instead of resisting, I lunged forward and bit her fingers. With a yelp, she released me. I ducked under her arm and darted past her along the narrow ledge.

Now I was at one end of the ledge and Julianne and Rick were at the other. Julianne was nearest me. She lunged for my arm again. Missed. With a huge roar, I reached out and shoved her in the chest. She stumbled backwards, her arms windmilling.

I turned and raced across the ledge. Behind me Julianne was screaming, but I didn't look back. I scrambled up the cliff side. There was no path on this side of the ledge, but I clutched at the dark stone ridges, forcing myself up.

I neared the top of the cliff. Julianne was still screaming. I glanced quickly around. She was hanging off the ledge, just one elbow hooked over the top. Rick had her arm and was pulling her up.

I didn't have much time. I hauled myself up. Up. The sharp edges of the rocks cut into my fingers. My trainers slid, then gripped, then slid again.

I reached the top of the cliff. I lay for a second, gasping for breath. There was no time to rest. I pulled myself across the ground, pressing my palms flat against the rough stone.

I took a breath and pushed myself up.

Which is when I saw his feet. I looked up, past his shoes, from his legs to his face.

He was standing over me, huge and macho, a look of surprise on his face.

Cooper Trent.

'I was coming to rescue you,' he said.

'Rescue me?' I scrambled to my feet.

He grabbed my arm. 'Out of the frying pan,' he said. 'Into the fire.'

20

A Bigger Fish

Before I knew what was happening, Cooper had forced me to the ground and bound my wrists with plastic ties. As I opened my mouth to scream, he slapped some duct tape over my face then reached down and bound my ankles together. His movements were swift and precise.

'Help!' My shriek was completely muffled.

'Stay there,' he ordered.

I struggled onto my knees as Cooper strode towards the edge of the cliff. Rick was racing up the path towards him. He stopped, blinking in the moonlight.

'Where's Frank?' Rick said.

'I killed him to stop him killing me.' Cooper's fists rammed into Rick's stomach. Left. Right. Left again.

His movements were unbelievably fast.

Rick staggered backwards into Julianne, who was following him up the path.

'What the hell are you doing, Cooper?' she shrieked, waving her gun at him. 'We told you you'd get a cut of the money. There was no need—'

Before Julianne could finish her sentence, Cooper knocked

the gun out of her hand. It sailed into the night air and disappeared behind the cliff.

Even before it splashed into the sea, Cooper had already turned to Rick again. His fist flew out. With a horrible crack, he made contact with Rick's chin. Rick flew backwards, landing with a groan out of sight.

Julianne raced after him. Cooper marched towards them both. My pulse thundered in my ears as he disappeared from view.

Cooper had obviously come back for the two million pounds. But what on earth was he going to do with me? I tried again to move, but it was impossible even to shuffle forwards with my feet tied so tightly.

Rick yelled out. Julianne screamed. I strained my eyes and ears towards the cliff edge and the ledge below.

For a few seconds there was silence, the only sound the rhythmic crashing of the waves on the rocks.

And then, into that silence, two distinct splashes sounded – one after the other.

My blood ran cold. I knew, though I hadn't seen it happen, that Cooper had thrown Rick and Julianne into the rocky sea, hundreds of metres below.

I also knew there was no way anyone could survive such a fall.

A moment later Cooper was back, flexing his fingers, the tote bag containing the two million pounds at his side.

'What are you going to do with me?' I asked, panic rising. My words came out all muffled and indistinct because of the gag, but I persisted, desperate for answers. 'Where are the others? Where are Jam and Madison and Shelby?'

Cooper said nothing. He wasn't even out of breath. He picked me up and put me over his shoulder as if I were an empty sack.

'Where are we going?' I shouted, bucking against him.

'Stop that!' He gripped me tighter so I could hardly breathe.

I writhed against him, trying to look around. The cliff top was as deserted as it had been earlier. Rick's car was parked just behind the van.

'Where are Jam and my sisters?' I yelled, my words still indistinct. 'What have you done with them?'

Cooper strode over to the car, deposited me on the ground and opened the boot. In the distance, a rumble of thunder sounded.

'In you go,' he said.

'No!' I scrabbled at the rough grass, trying to claw myself away from him. 'HELP!' I was yelling at the top of my lungs, but my voice could barely be heard from behind the gag over my mouth.

I hurled my body across the grass. But it was hopeless. With a sigh, Cooper took a cloth from his pocket. He picked me up again. I bucked once more, trying to loosen his grip, but he was too strong. A moment later the cloth was over my nose. A sickly sweet smell filled my nostrils. I tried not to breathe, but it was impossible.

As Cooper laid me inside the boot, my head spun. And then the world went black.

* * *

148

'Lauren? Lauren, are you OK?' It was Madison's voice. 'Her eyelids are moving, Jam. I think she's waking up.'

I struggled to open my eyes, but the effort was too much.

'Lauren?' As Jam spoke, I felt a hand on my forehead, stroking the hair off my face.

I tried to speak – at least my mouth was no longer gagged – but all that came out was a splutter of air.

'It's OK,' Jam said. 'You're OK. We're all here. Me, Madison and Shelby.'

'And we called Mommy too,' Madison added. 'That big man let me speak to her . . . he made me make her promise not to go to the police. He said we'd be home by morning. Then he took all our phones away.'

I struggled to speak again, to point out there was no way we could trust anything Cooper Trent promised. This time I managed something that sounded like a cross between a whimper and a moan.

'D'you think she's hurt, Jam?' Madison said anxiously. I felt her small fingers reach for my hand.

'No.' Jam's voice sounded closer than before. 'No, I think she's probably trying to tell us that what Cooper says and what he means are two different things.'

I smiled to myself. Jam had always understood me better than anyone. With a horrible jolt, I remembered how he'd been kidnapped earlier because I'd been so selfish and obstinate.

'Oh, Jam,' I said, managing a soft whisper.

'Yeah?' His voice was right by my ear.

'I'm so sorry you got taken. It was all my fault.' Tears pricked at my eyes. I'd been worried before that Jam was only with me because he felt he should be. But now it struck me that no-one could blame him if he *did* dump me. Not only was I difficult – as he had often pointed out – but I was also a magnet for life-threatening danger.

I opened my eyes. Jam's face was right next to mine, his hazel eyes soft and smiling.

'Don't sweat it, Lazerbrain,' he said. 'Feeling sorry for yourself was never your best look.'

'At least I have a best look.' I attempted to speak properly as I smiled, but my throat was too dry and it came out as a croak. I was lying on hard, cold ground, though someone had slipped something soft under my head. My head ached a little and I was very thirsty, but otherwise I didn't feel too bad.

I squeezed Madison's hand.

'Lauren?' Madison's face loomed over mine, her brown eyes huge and full of concern. I got a whiff of her sweet, strawberry breath.

'Hey, sweetheart,' I rasped. It was unbelievably good to see her. 'Are you all right?'

'Yes.' She hugged me.

I looked round. Jam was on my other side. He sat back on his heels. 'Headache?'

I winced. 'Yeah.'

'We're the same,' Jam said. 'Cooper drugged all of us in the car before we drove off.'

I nodded. That made sense. Jam, Madison and Shelby must have already been in the back seat of the car when Cooper bundled me into the boot. I'd been too busy trying to fight him off to have noticed.

I struggled onto my elbows and looked round. We were in a large basement room: bare, white walls, a grubby, threadbare carpet on the floor and no natural light whatsoever. There was no furniture other than a couple of plastic chairs stacked in one corner. A bare electric bulb hung from the ceiling. Jam and Madison were sitting on either side of me. Jam's jumper was the soft material I'd felt under my head.

I twisted round. Shelby was hunched in the far corner of the room. She stared at me with miserable, angry eyes.

'Where are we?' I said, rubbing the back of my head. I still felt groggy, but my head was clearing.

'No idea,' Jam said. 'We all came round in this room, same as you.'

'At least we're not tied up any more,' Madison said, cuddling up next to me.

I put my arm round her. It was true. The plastic strips round my wrists and ankles were gone.

'I'm thirsty,' I said.

'Me too,' Madison said.

'Have you tried calling for help?'

Jam made a face. 'Yeah. The three of us yelled our heads off for about five minutes. Nothing happened.'

'Except we got thirstier,' Madison said ruefully.

A lock turned in the door.

151

I scrambled to my feet, pushing Madison behind me. Jam stood up too. Together, we faced the door as it opened.

Cooper Trent stood, huge and menacing, in the doorway. I hadn't realised how muscular he was until right now. His biceps bulged under his T-shirt. His hair was wet and slicked back from his face, as if he'd just stepped out of the shower, and the handle of a knife protruded from his jeans pocket.

'Good, you're all awake.' He smiled. 'You were only out for about twenty minutes, so the headaches shouldn't last long.'

I glanced at Jam. I knew he was considering the same thing that I was – could we get past Cooper and make a run for it?

But another glance and I realised how hopeless our position was. Cooper was armed, and far, far bigger even than Jam. On top of that, I'd seen on the cliff top how fast the man could move, despite his bulk. I'd also seen how lethal his attacks were – and how ruthless.

'You killed Rick and the people he was working with,' I blurted out.

I could feel Jam and Madison stiffen beside me. Of course, they hadn't seen the cliff top struggle.

Cooper raised an eyebrow. 'Those amateur losers?' He gave a dismissive shrug. 'They got what they deserved. That's what happens to small fish who try to swim in a big pond.'

'You being, like, a bigger fish, I suppose?' I said.

Cooper grinned. 'There's always a bigger fish, Lauren.'

'Why are we here?' Jam asked.

'Yeah, you've got the two million. What do you want with us?' I added.

Shelby walked over and stood on Jam's other side. 'Where are we anyway?' she said, trying to look fierce by putting her hands on her hips and jutting out her chin. 'Who the hell *are* you?'

Cooper Trent's smile broadened. 'So many questions,' he said. 'Well, just for your information, I used to work in kidnap and ransom. That part of what Rick told you was true. And I'm ex-army. Special forces. Though I haven't had what you'd call a conventional job for quite a while. Right now you're in the basement of my rented house.'

'What are you going to do with us?' I asked.

'You said it was OK to tell our mom we'd be home by morning,' Madison said.

I put my arm round her and squeezed her shoulder.

'If all goes according to plan then you *will* be home by morning,' Cooper said. He turned to me. 'It depends on you, Lauren, whether the rest of them turn up there dead or alive.'

Madison gasped.

My guts clenched. 'What d'you mean it depends on me?'

'I mean,' Cooper said, 'that there's something I want you to do tonight, Lauren. And everybody else's lives depend on whether you succeed or fail.'

21

A New Plan

Silence fell in the basement room.

I stared up at Cooper Trent's rugged, relaxed face. He was smiling at our confusion. Apart from the knife handle poking out of his jeans pocket, he looked more like someone's slightly wild uncle than a man who had just murdered three people and announced that everyone's lives depended on me carrying out his orders tonight.

'What do you want me to do?' I touched the wooden oval round my neck. Normally this made me feel calmer, but not now.

Nothing was going to calm me down right now.

Cooper leaned against the wall behind him and folded his arms. 'When Rick first told me – *boasted* to me – about how he was fooling your mother by pretending to kidnap your sister—'

'I *was* kidnapped,' Madison protested, peering out from behind me. Her voice was defiant, but I could feel her fists against my back as she gripped my jumper.

Cooper shrugged. 'Anyway, when Rick and I spoke, he was full of himself for pulling off the whole stunt, making Lauren think the kidnapper was Sonia Holtwood.'

I glared at him, not wanting to admit how easily I had been fooled.

'Rick said he had your mother wound round his little finger . . .' Cooper went on. 'He told me how he'd manipulated the situation so that he was about to get two million pounds. Then he explained about the cock-up with the first exchange and how his stupid girlfriend – that Julianne – had tried, and failed, to raise the stakes by sending you after non-existent valuables. And I saw that for all his big talk he had no idea what he was doing.'

'So you thought you'd muscle in and take the money for yourself,' Jam said in a disgusted voice.

'At first that was all I planned,' Cooper admitted. 'But then I found something . . .'

He drew a piece of folded paper out of his pocket.

'Recognise this?' he asked Jam.

I looked at Jam. His eyes widened with shock. He put his hands in his own pockets. But it was obvious his jeans were empty.

With a terrible jolt, I realised that what Cooper held in his hand was Sam's letter to Shelby. I glanced round at her. She was frowning, clearly confused.

My throat tightened. That letter was a bomb. I didn't much like Shelby, but I wouldn't want my worst enemy finding out the truth about her parents like this.

'Don't,' Jam said. 'Please.'

'What is that?' Shelby asked.

Madison shuffled even closer to me. At least the other

letter, explaining that she, like me, had been fathered by an anonymous sperm donor, was still safely back at the holiday home.

'Ah, you don't know about this, Shelby,' Cooper said softly. He paused for a second.

'*I* know what's in that letter,' I said quickly. 'And you said this was all about something *I* have to do, so you don't need to read it to everyone.'

'Don't you think Shelby has a right to know what this letter says, Lauren?' Cooper raised his eyebrows.

I said nothing.

There was nothing I could say.

And then Cooper Trent read the letter out loud.

I stared at the floor, my face burning. I couldn't look at Jam, I couldn't look at Shelby.

As Cooper read, the atmosphere in the room grew tense.

'So you see,' Cooper said, handing the letter to Shelby, 'your *real* father is Simeon Duchovny.'

I glanced round at Shelby. She was staring open-mouthed at the letter. I caught Jam's eye. He looked as desperate as I felt.

And yet it was my fault that Shelby was finding out this way that her mother had had an affair and Sam wasn't her birth dad. Jam had wanted to tell her immediately.

I should have listened to him.

Shelby was reading the letter again.

I had read and reread mine. It still hadn't sunk in that Sam wasn't my birth father, but at least I knew Annie and Sam had *chosen* together to use an anonymous sperm donor . . . that I hadn't been conceived out of mistrust and betrayal.

Shelby looked up at Jam. 'I can't believe you've been carrying this around,' she said.

'I'm sorry.' Jam stared at the ground.

Shelby shook her head. 'You're the most disgusting person I've ever met.'

'That's not fair.' I stormed over, forgetting that Cooper Trent was still in the room. 'Jam *wanted* to show you. I asked him to wait. I wanted—'

'Then *you're* the most disgusting person I've ever met,' Shelby spat. 'But I guess I already knew that.'

We glared at each other. My heart was pounding in my chest. How *dare* Shelby talk to me like that?

'You stupid—' I started.

'Stop it, Lauren,' Jam said firmly. 'Shelby's just upset.'

I turned away, my cheeks burning. Cooper Trent was watching me, an expression of interested amusement on his face.

Shelby retreated to the far corner of the room. I took a deep breath.

'I don't get this,' I said. 'What's Shelby's birth dad – this Simeon Duchovny guy – got to do with me and why we're here?'

Cooper Trent straightened up, assuming a more business-like air.

'Don't you guys know who Simeon Duchovny is?' he said.

'Never heard of him,' Jam said.

I glanced at Shelby again. She was now looking intently at Cooper. Her face was pale and her expression still bewildered.

157

'Simeon Duchovny is one of the richest men in England,' Cooper said. 'He made a fortune in the late nineties with some dot.com business, then went into merchant banking. He's got a fine art collection worth millions. Man, *he* is worth millions.'

'I still don't get it,' I said. 'What's that got to do with me?'

Cooper glanced from me to Shelby and back again.

'She's your sister, Lauren,' he said. 'Isn't it obvious?'

The car drew to a crawl as we reached Duchovny's road. I had no idea where we were – Cooper had blindfolded me for most of the journey – but it was somewhere ultra posh. Each deluxe mansion we passed was bigger than the last. We stopped about twenty metres away from a gate at the end of a long curving driveway.

'This is Duchovny's place,' Cooper said. 'The house is along the drive.'

I peered past the gate and line of trees, searching for signs of a building . . . and the attendant security guards. Cooper had explained there would be an army of staff waiting on Duchovny's every need. And I was supposed to march right up to them and demand to see him.

I felt sick as Cooper unlocked the car doors.

'Ready, Lauren?'

'I don't think I can do this,' I said.

Cooper rolled his eyes. 'Of course you can. I saw you on that cliff edge. You're determined, ruthless and resourceful. You're perfect for the job.'

I shook my head.

'Anyway, once you've found Duchovny it's going to be plain sailing.'

I wasn't at all sure that was true. Not that Cooper's plan wasn't simple. It was . . . *ridiculously* simple: he wanted me to meet with Duchovny and ask for a ransom for Shelby.

'But he may not even know Shelby's his daughter,' I'd said.

'Of course he knows,' Cooper had chuckled. 'I spoke to your mother earlier. Forced her to tell me the whole story. Duchovny has been paying maintenance for your sister ever since she was born. Small amounts every month.' He paused. 'Now go on, get out of my car and speak to him.'

I walked over to the gate and pressed the buzzer. Moments later a security guard appeared. He was dressed in a dark blue uniform with a walkie-talkie hanging from his belt. As soon as he saw me, he strode over and peered at me through the bars.

'Yes?' he said, unsmiling.

I gulped. 'Please tell Mr Duchovny that I'm here.'

The guard frowned. 'Is he expecting you?'

'No,' I said.

'Go on, Lauren,' Cooper's voice hissed in my ear. 'Say what I told you to say.'

I looked the guard in the eye. 'Tell Mr Duchovny I'm here about . . . about Shelby.'

Keeping me in his sights, the guard backed a few paces away. His radio crackled as he picked it up. He spoke into it, passing on my message.

Another crackle.

And the voice through the other end.

Mr Duchovny says bring her round the back. Film room.

'Over and out.' The security guard let me through the gate, then took a hand scanner from his belt and waved it up and down my body. It emitted a series of gentle beeps. The guard put the scanner away.

'This way,' he said, turning on his heel and striding across the gravel.

Shoving my trembling hands in my pockets, I followed him.

I desperately wished Jam was with me. Not that I was really sure any more that Jam *wanted* to be with me. Earlier, at Cooper's house, there hadn't been time for intimacies until the moment I left. At that point, Madison had hugged me fiercely, like she always did, but Jam had seemed cooler than usual, just telling me to be careful and giving me a quick kiss.

Maybe he was starting to count all the ways I'd let him down. Shelby's outburst had been so unfair – especially after how I'd messed up myself. Maybe Jam was starting to wonder why on earth he stayed with me when it led to so much danger and aggravation.

I shook myself. I couldn't worry about that now.

I followed the security guard round the bend in the drive. An enormous, modern three-storey house made of brick and glass came into view. It was as big as it was intimidating.

For a second, now I was out of Cooper's eyeline, I was tempted to throw myself on the guard's mercy and beg him to protect me while I called the police and told them everything. But there was no point. Cooper still had me exactly where he wanted me. The lives of the other three were at stake.

As if to remind me of his presence, Cooper chose that moment to make contact.

'Nearly there, Lauren?' He spoke through the earpiece he'd given me. No bigger than a tiny stud earring, this device meant he could both hear what I said and speak privately to me.

The fact that Cooper had such devices so easily to hand seemed, like everything else he'd done so far, to reinforce his own assertion that he was in a different league to Rick and the original kidnappers.

'I'm right outside,' I whispered.

'Get on with it then,' Cooper said.

I followed the guard towards the house.

22

Simeon Duchovny

'Over there.' The guard indicated the rear of the house. I hesitated. Whereas the front of the building was well lit, the back was in shadow. 'Come on,' he said.

As I followed him, I realised just how massive the house was. What I'd taken to be the back was, in fact, simply a brick wall marking the end of the main part of the mansion and the start of a long, low extension. The guard led me past the ground lights that ran down the side of the building to a reinforced glass door. Two plant pots stood on either side of it. Even in the dark, everything felt very manicured and expensive.

The guard inserted a key card into the lock. A green light flashed on and he pushed the door open. The inside of the house was as minimalist and smart as the outside – all soft lighting and elegant modern furniture.

The guard took me along a carpeted corridor and down a flight of steps. Another corridor. A series of abstract oil paintings lined the walls. I remembered Cooper's comment about Duchovny's art collection being worth millions and stared at the pictures. I'd done a huge project on both Kraminsky and Stutter for my Art GCSE and recognised works by both as I walked past.

If they were originals they were worth a fortune.

We reached a large wooden door. The guard pushed it open and stood back to let me through.

'Wait here,' he said.

As I walked in, he closed the door behind me. I was alone in what appeared to be some kind of home cinema. Three rows of squashy armchairs were ranged in front of a large screen hung on the far wall. I walked round the room. Signed prints of various celebrities – only some of whom I recognised – hung on the walls. A locked cupboard ran the length of one wall.

The room smelled of furniture polish and popcorn.

Footsteps sounded outside and, a second later, the door opened and a short stocky man with sharp grey eyes walked in. I didn't have to ask if it was Duchovny. The way the security guard stepped back, almost bowing his head as the man passed him, said it all. And Duchovny radiated power, despite being only a couple of centimetres taller than I was. His suit – dark and sharply cut over a pale green, open-necked shirt – fitted him perfectly and he held himself very upright, from his polished shoes to his grey-streaked hair. But it was his expression that was most striking. He looked at me as if I were some kind of bug. Interesting, yes, but lowly. Very lowly.

'What do you want?' His accent was clipped . . . English, with an American twang.

I gulped, then spoke as Cooper had directed me to, using information from Sam's letter:

'I'm here because of Shelby,' I said. 'You had an affair with her mother, Annie, fifteen years ago. Shelby's your daughter, as . . . as you know. You pay money to Annie for her every month.'

Duchovny's expression didn't alter, but a muscle twitched in his jaw. 'Shelby?' he said.

I wasn't sure if this was just some shorthand version of the question he was really asking, as in *why are you coming here talking about my illegitimate daughter?* but I launched into my prepared explanation of our kidnap, saying immediately why the kidnapper (Cooper had insisted I didn't use his name) had sent me.

'He wants five million pounds transferred to his bank account within the next thirty minutes,' I finished.

Duchovny frowned. 'And *you're* Shelby?'

'No.' I shook my head. 'No. She's my sister. I mean we didn't grow up together, but—'

'Slow down, Lauren. Just tell him what he needs to know,' Cooper's menacing voice hissed in my ear.

I stopped speaking. Duchovny narrowed his eyes.

'You're *Martha Lauren*?' he said. 'The elder daughter? The one who was found a couple of years ago?'

I nodded. There was a long pause. I searched Duchovny's face for signs of similarity to Shelby. Their eye-colour was definitely alike – and there was something about the shape of his mouth: the way the top lip dipped. She had his build, too, I realised – those same short legs.

I thought of Shelby and Jam and Madison waiting for me back in that basement. I had no idea how far away Cooper's

164

house was or in which direction – though we'd driven for over an hour to get here – but I knew their lives were in my hands.

Duchovny cleared his throat. 'One of my conditions with Annie is that Shelby – that *nobody* – would ever know the truth about her being my daughter.'

'This is good, Lauren, he's not even attempting to deny it,' Cooper hissed in my ear.

'Annie told Sam, her . . . her husband who died. And Sam wrote us letters. I mean, he's dead but he wrote us letters before—'

'I'm not interested in the details.' Duchovny's voice was as cold as his eyes. 'I made it quite clear to Annie many years ago that while I would make a reasonable financial contribution towards a situation I helped create, I was not prepared to go further.'

I stared at him. In all the upheaval of the past few hours it hadn't occurred to me that unlike my anonymous sperm donor father, who *couldn't* know who I was, Duchovny had made a deliberate choice not to know his daughter.

'Shelby's not a "situation",' I said. 'She's a person. She's . . . jeez, you're her *father*. Doesn't that matter to you?'

Duchovny's eyes were like steel.

'No,' he said. 'It doesn't matter to me. Shelby is *nothing* to me . . . she's just an annoying reminder of an irresponsible period a long time ago.'

My mouth gaped. 'That's horrible,' I said.

Cooper swore violently in my ear. *'Stay on track, Lauren. Don't rile him.'*

165

Duchovny raised an eyebrow. 'Shelby's mother had a husband who was prepared to accept the baby as his own. I had a wife and a son, neither of whom have ever needed to know of Shelby's existence. I've done my duty to clear up the mess I made. My responsibility goes no further.' He paused. 'Now I'd like you to leave.'

Cooper swore again in my ear. *'Tell him you'll tell the wife.'*

'If you don't pay the ransom, we'll tell your wife about Shelby,' I said.

'A minute ago you said if I didn't pay the ransom then Shelby would die,' Duchovny snapped. 'Whoever sent you hasn't done their homework very well if they think I'm the sort of person who can be blackmailed. So let me make this clear: I don't care what you tell to whom. I don't care about Shelby *at all*.'

He opened the door.

I had no choice but to walk through it.

'Don't let this happen, Lauren,' Cooper hissed.

'What the hell do you want me to do?' The words – meant for Cooper – burst out of me. Duchovny clearly thought I'd been speaking to him. He curled his lip.

'I want you to leave, now, and never come back.' He beckoned to the security guard who had been waiting outside the room. As the man walked towards us, his jacket flapped open and I noticed a gun, nestling in its holster against his chest.

'Make sure she leaves the premises,' Duchovny ordered.

'No,' I said.

'Do something,' Cooper insisted in my ear.

166

Duchovny turned and walked away along the corridor.

'Come on,' the guard said, indicating the way out which was in the opposite direction.

'No,' I said again.

'Do something, Lauren!' Cooper's voice rumbled inside my head. *'Do something or Jam and your sisters die.'*

I had no idea what to do.

Without thinking it through, I lunged forward and thrust my knee up, hard, between the guard's legs.

He doubled over. I reached for his gun. It slid, easily, out of the holster. I jumped backwards, the gun in my hand. The metal felt cold against my palm.

Beyond me, along the corridor, Duchovny was still walking away.

I took a deep breath. 'Stop!' I demanded. 'Stop or I'll shoot.'

23

The Ransom

The guard looked up, his eyes filling with horror. He took a step away from me. I glanced over at Duchovny who had stopped walking and was turning slowly around to face me.

'Transfer the money or I'll shoot you,' I said.

My voice was steady with a steel edge. I should have been scared, but the gun in my hand made me feel powerful.

So did the look of fear on the guard's face.

'Have you taken his gun, Lauren?' Cooper swore in my ear.

'Put that down before you hurt yourself.' Unlike the guard, Duchovny's expression was full of contempt.

My resolution faltered.

'Shoot the guard. Get Duchovny alone,' Cooper hissed.

My head spun. Was he seriously telling me to pull the trigger? I gulped.

'Throw me the key card and get back,' I ordered the guard. At least if I had the key card I could get out of here.

The guard unclipped his key card and slid it across the floor to me. He put his hands up and stepped back against the wall. Keeping the gun trained on him, I bent down and picked up the key card.

168

'For goodness' sake, she's a child,' Duchovny spat. 'She doesn't know how to use that gun. Go and get it.'

'Lauren, stand up to him!' Cooper insisted. *'Get them both to back off.'*

'Shut up!' I said.

I held the gun in both hands, my arms outstretched. I swung it from the guard to Duchovny and back again, past the rows of oil paintings along the corridor wall.

'Get the gun off her,' Duchovny ordered the guard again.

The guard hesitated, but I could tell he was going to obey the order. I only had a few seconds before he rushed over.

And I knew, in my heart, I would never be able to pull the trigger.

Duchovny swore. He started walking towards me.

'Lauren!' Cooper shouted.

I felt sick with fear. Somehow I had to take Cooper a ransom – *and* get out of here alive. I had no idea what to do.

And then I noticed the picture on the wall opposite. It was a Stutter, I was sure. Really similar to one I'd written about for my Art GCSE. About half a metre square: an abstract oil painting consisting of three blue stripes.

It was bound to be worth millions.

There was no time to think. Duchovny had almost reached the guard. In a single movement I darted forward, yanked the painting off the wall and raced for the stairs. I climbed them two at a time, then tore along the corridor to the door.

'Stop!' the guard yelled. He was right behind me.

169

I slid the key card over the lock. The reinforced glass door popped open. I ran through as the guard and Duchovny raced up. I slammed the door in their faces and slid the key card over the lock again. A red light came on.

Duchovny rammed his shoulder against the door, but it held firm. He was yelling at the guard to open it. The guard was protesting that he couldn't because I'd taken his key card.

I dropped the gun and the key card and tore down the drive, the oil painting under my arm.

I flew along the track, my legs barely touching the path.

'What the hell are you doing?' Cooper was shouting in my ear.

'I'm coming!' I panted. 'Get the car ready!'

A second later I turned the corner on the drive. I could hear shouts now coming from outside the house. Duchovny was ordering his men to chase me.

I sped up, my breath rasping at my throat. I pushed my legs on. Further. Faster. The gate came into view. I reached it. Pressed the release button. The doors swung open. I raced through.

Cooper was standing outside his car. He saw me running and got inside. As I hurled myself into the passenger seat, he revved the engine. We sped off, the car screeching down the road.

'What did you do?' Cooper glanced at the painting. 'What the hell is that?'

'It's your ransom,' I gasped. 'Duchovny wasn't going to give you any money. So I took this instead. It's an original Stutter. At least I think it is.'

Cooper swung the car round a corner. Then another. He swerved off the road and skidded the car to a stop. I had no idea where we were.

Cooper reached over and took the painting off my lap.

'If I'd wanted a piece of art I'd have gone to a freakin' gallery.' He swore. 'This is probably a reproduction anyway. Now get under the blanket on the back seat so I can drive home.'

I hesitated. I wanted to fight him. To get away. But Cooper was far more powerful than I was – and he still had his knife.

'Are Madison and the others OK?' I asked.

'They're where we left them,' Cooper snapped. 'Now get in the back.'

As I lay on the back seat, Cooper covered my mouth with a damp cloth. I smelled the same sickly scent as I had back on the cliff top.

'No,' I started to protest. But before I'd even finished speaking, I'd lost consciousness.

I came to back in the basement. I blinked open my eyes, looking round for the others as soon as I could move.

But I was alone.

Panic gripped me.

What had Cooper done with Jam and my sisters?

'Hey!' I struggled to my feet and hammered on the door. 'Hey! Let me out!'

But no-one came.

I had no idea what time it was. Back at Duchovny's house I'd had a strong sense that it was late evening. But I didn't know how long I'd been unconscious, and I couldn't see outside – the only light in the basement came from the single bulb that hung from the middle of the ceiling.

Time crept by. I was getting more and more afraid. Suppose Cooper was just going to leave me here to die?

I hadn't had anything to eat or drink since . . . jeez, I couldn't remember when. I felt light-headed and my head ached. I wanted to cry, but the terror inside me was like a fist gripping me, holding on too tight for me to let go and give in to my misery.

And then, without warning, Cooper unlocked the door. He looked tired. There were shadows under his eyes and signs of fresh stubble on his chin.

'Time to go,' he said, shortly.

'Where are the others?' I said.

'Already there.'

'Where?'

Cooper shook his head impatiently. He tapped the knife attached to his belt. 'Come on,' he ordered. 'They're waiting.'

Heart thumping, I followed him out of the basement room. He gripped my arm and led me along the bare corridor and up a flight of stairs.

I looked round, bewildered. The house sounded empty . . . almost eerie. Was Cooper really taking me to the others?

'Are you letting us go?' I asked. 'Is that Stutter worth a lot?'

'We're moving to Plan B,' Cooper said, ignoring my question. 'Through here.'

172

We'd reached the top of the stairs and were standing in some sort of utility room. There was a boiler and a washing machine and a sink in the far corner. Cooper indicated a door that led outside to a dark garden. I could just make out the outline of a tree against the night sky.

I stared at him.

'We're going outside?' I said.

'You're a genius,' Cooper said sarcastically.

He pushed the door open and I stumbled out. The air was cold and damp, like it was about to rain. A strong, salt smell drifted on the wind across the garden. It took me a moment to realise that the garden led down to a jetty and that the sea – pitch black – lay beyond.

Cooper prodded me towards the jetty. A boat was moored at one end.

I looked round. The garden was lined on both sides by trees. The house was completely isolated – no other buildings in the distance.

'Where are we going?' I said.

Cooper said nothing. We reached the jetty. Our steps sounded loud on the wooden slats.

'Get in the boat,' Cooper ordered.

'No,' I said, backing away. 'Why?'

'I told you already.' Cooper grabbed my arm. Somehow his knife was already in the other hand. He held it to my throat. 'The others are waiting for you. Get in the boat.'

I had no choice. Trembling, I stepped into the wooden motor boat. It wasn't large – just room for one person at the front and two at the back, by the engine. Cooper sat me down beside him and started the engine.

We motored out to sea. The spray was fine and cold against my face. I shivered in my jumper. I thought about jumping overboard and trying to swim back to dry land, but I knew how powerful the currents were here. Anyway, within seconds, the shore was just a distant bank of lights.

After a few more minutes, Cooper changed course. We motored along, parallel to the shore, for a while. Gradually the bank of lights dwindled to darkness. I could just make out waves breaking at the base of a stretch of deserted cliff.

'What are we doing here?' I said. 'Where are the others?'

Cooper didn't reply. He turned off the engine. The boat rocked gently in the water. Waves slapped at the hull.

'Get out,' he ordered.

I stared at him, my pulse racing.

'What?'

'You heard.' Cooper's fingers curled round the knife at his side.

'You want me to get into the sea?' I said.

The water below me was dark as the night sky above.

'If you don't get in I'll throw you in,' Cooper said.

'No.' I scrabbled away from him, towards the front of the boat.

In a second he'd lunged after me, grabbing my arm and twisting it round my back.

I kicked out, my shoes thudding against the hull.

'No!' I screamed. 'NO!'

'Shut up.' Cooper's knife pricked at my throat.

'Is this what you did to the others?' I froze, the full horror of the situation dawning on me.

Cooper had dumped Jam and Madison and Shelby into the water too. They were already dead. Drowned.

Cooper said nothing. Still keeping the knife at my throat, he put his other arm round my waist and lifted me over the side of the boat. My legs dangled in the air for a second then, with a grunt, Cooper hurled me into the water.

It was ice-cold. I sank, the water consuming me for a few seconds. I clawed my way back to the surface, gasping for air. Salt waves splashed over my face. My arms and legs were already sodden, weighed down by my clothes and shoes. Automatically, instinctively, I began treading water.

The boat's engine revved. Cooper motored away, the boat leaving a white trail in the water. In seconds it had disappeared into the darkness. Stunned, I watched the foam disperse.

Silence fell over the sea. Apart from the swish of the waves there was, literally, no sound. I looked around. From where I was, low down in the water, I could make out neither coast properly, but the current seemed to be tugging me to the right. I moved my arms and legs, going with the water, letting it guide me.

Images flashed in front of my eyes. Mum calling from Disney World, not understanding why I didn't answer . . . why I hadn't called back . . . Jam and my sisters . . . all drowned . . . their bodies sinking in this sea. Annie losing all of us . . . A sob rose up inside me. *No*. I couldn't let myself think about it.

My eyes stung from the salt but I strained them, looking for some landmark to head for. The moon came out from behind a cloud and, for the first time, I saw the pale beach spread out in front of me.

I started swimming towards it. I had no idea how far away it was. The current swirled around me, pulling me sideways as well as towards the shore. I struggled against the sideways motion. I had to keep that beach in my sights. It was horse-shoe-shaped – a bay set into high cliffs that rose out of the land and seemed to loom above me: dark and smooth and sinister.

The current tugged at my legs. It was strong and I felt weak. Weak from lack of food. Weak from fear. Would I make it to the shore? Could I possibly survive this long, cold, terrifying swim?

Freezing waves slapped against my face. As I pushed myself on, all my focus on the undulating coastline ahead, a human figure rose up from the sand.

My heart constricted in my chest.

There was someone on the beach.

24

Trapped

I stopped swimming for a second. Immediately I felt the current tug at me, threatening to sweep me sideways, out of the bay and into the dark sea beyond.

The deep chill was seeping through my bones. *If you stay in the water you will die.* The thought was as clear as the cold all around me. I kicked my legs against it, pushing on to the shore.

Better to face whoever was on the beach than to die in the sea.

I pulled my arms through the waves. Another stroke. Another kick. Another. For a few terrifying seconds, it felt like I was only treading water – that the shore was as far away as when Cooper had tipped me off the boat – and then I clawed at the water and kicked and my foot touched the bottom. Another few strokes and the seabed was properly under my feet. I stood up, water rushing off me. The wind was fierce on my skin, but the sea only came up to my thighs. I pushed on, letting the waves break against the backs of my legs. I was still some distance from the shore. The figure on the beach was standing directly in front of me – a dark smudge against the sand.

177

'Lauren! Is that you?' The voice was faint, battling against the crash of the waves and the rush of the wind, but it was as familiar to me as my own.

Relief surged through me.

'Jam!' I tried to call back, but my voice croaked with exhaustion.

I waded on. The going was easier now, despite the cold wind that whipped around me, plastering my clothes and hair to my body.

Jam stood at the edge of the sea, waiting for me. I forced my legs on, through the water. And at last I was there, stumbling through the last stretch of sea and onto the damp sand. I sank into Jam's arms and he hugged me fiercely back.

'Thank goodness you're all right,' he said.

'Where's Madison?' I gasped. 'What about Shelby?'

'Madison's over there asleep.' Jam pointed across the beach to where the cliff jutted out, offering a little shelter from the wind. 'Shelby's still back at Cooper's house. Didn't you see her?'

'No.' Tears of relief rushed into my eyes. It was bad that Shelby wasn't here too, but at least I had Jam and Madison back – and now we could get home . . . go to the police . . . which meant Jam and I wouldn't have to hold everything together for too much longer.

'Oh, Jam. Please don't leave me. Please don't go.' The words came from nowhere, sobbing out of me.

He pulled away from me so he could see my face.

'Leave you?' he frowned. 'What on earth are you talking about?'

'Nothing.' I looked down, suddenly embarrassed that I'd sounded so desperate.

Everything's going to be OK now.

I fixed my gaze on the damp sand at my feet. Jam's hand curled under my chin, lifting it up.

Jam's hair was plastered against his forehead, his clothes wet, his body shivering. I looked at the strong lines of his face and his eyes, all warm with concern, and I felt a rush of love for him, as strong as the love I felt for Madison.

'What did you mean?' Jam said. 'Why did you think I might leave you?'

Oh, man. 'I wasn't sure how you felt any more,' I stuttered, through chattering teeth. 'I've messed up so badly and got you into so much danger . . .'

'Well, that's true . . .' Jam raised his eyebrows.

I laughed and cried and shivered all at once. 'And . . . and before that,' I stammered, remembering how he'd pulled away from our kiss before. 'Well, I wasn't sure if you really wanted to be with me.'

Jam's eyes widened. 'I wasn't sure if *you* wanted to be with *me*,' he said. 'Sometimes you act like you don't care, Lauren.' He paused. 'Not just with me. With everyone.'

Was that true?

I guess sometimes I did pull away from people. It was part of being strong and independent. Wasn't it?

'I'm sorry,' I said.

179

Jam hugged me again. 'You are the stupidest person I've ever met,' he whispered. 'I'm not going to leave you. Don't you know that I love you?'

I whispered the words back, forgetting everything else, even how cold I was.

Jam pulled back and looked at me again. 'Anyway, I can't leave you,' he said, his lips stretching into a rueful smile. 'We're stuck on this beach.'

'What?' I looked round, taking in the little bay properly for the first time. The rocks that rose out of the beach were certainly sheer, but surely there must be some way to climb them.

'I've been right round the bay,' Jam explained. 'Cooper knew what he was doing, dumping us here. All the rocks are straight up and down. No footholds.'

'You mean the only way out of the bay is through the sea?' I said.

Jam looked out across the water. He lowered his voice. 'I haven't said anything to Madison, obviously, but I'm really worried. We're wet and cold. None of us have had anything to eat or drink since this morning. And the current's too strong for us to swim round the bay.'

I nodded. All this was true.

'Maybe we can signal to a passing ship when it's daylight,' I said.

We walked across the beach towards the spot where Madison lay. As we drew closer to the cliff face, I could see that Jam was right. The rocks rising up from the beach were tall and smooth – there was no way to climb any of them.

'What about Shelby?' I said. 'Why does Cooper still have her?'

'I guess he thinks Duchovny's bluffing about not paying a ransom,' Jam said. 'He's probably going to ask for money again.'

'But I stole the painting . . . the Stutter,' I protested. 'That's worth millions, it *must* be.'

Jam shrugged. 'Maybe it's not as valuable as you thought. Or maybe it wasn't a Stutter.'

I frowned. I was sure I'd been right about that.

We reached Madison. She was lying on the sand, curled up and fast asleep. I dropped to my knees and touched her hand. She was frozen. I pulled her to me, hoping my body heat – not that there was much of that – would warm her up. As I moved her, she opened her eyes.

'Hey, Lauren.' She smiled up at me. 'Me and Jam swam to the beach.'

I glanced at Jam. I could only imagine how close they had come to drowning. I had no doubt that, on her own, Madison would certainly not have made it.

'I know, sweetheart,' I whispered. 'Everything's going to be OK now. We'll get away from here when it's daylight and we'll take you to Mommy and get the police to rescue Shelby.'

Madison put her arms around me and I held her close. She was shivering badly so I rubbed her arms to warm her up.

'Come and sit with us, Jam,' I said. 'We can keep each other warm.'

Jam sat on Madison's other side and the three of us huddled together on the damp sand. The way the rock stuck out in front stopped the worst of the wind, but a fierce breeze still blew round it, piercing right through us. I was soaking wet and the cliff at my back was cold and hard. After a few minutes, Madison stopped shivering. That was something. Having Jam and I on either side of her was clearly helping keep some of the cold out.

'This is just like two years ago,' she said softly. 'When Jam rescued us off Sonia Holtwood's boat.'

I cast my mind back to that horrible night and how we'd nearly drowned.

'But who's going to rescue us now?' Madison went on.

'We'll wait 'til it's light, then we'll wave at the ships that go by. One of them's bound to see us,' I said.

'Yeah, the sea round here is like Piccadilly Circus,' Jam added with fake cheeriness. 'In the daytime you can't *move* for all the boats.'

Madison giggled. 'Hey, Lauren, I wish we had some burgers.'

'Yeah, me too,' I said. 'I'd even go for one of Mommy's carrot-stick sandwiches.'

Jam made a face. 'I wouldn't.'

Madison giggled again.

We sat, huddled together, for what felt like ages. After a while, Madison fell back to sleep and I told Jam everything that had happened at Duchovny's house.

'Do you think you could have fired that gun?' he asked.

The wind had died down a little now, though the sound of the sea lapping at the beach seemed louder than before. I stared at the rock we were sheltering behind for a moment before replying.

'No,' I said. 'I don't think I could have done, even with everyone's lives being at stake.' I paused. I didn't want Jam to think badly of my cowardice. 'D'you think that means there's something wrong with me?'

Jam leaned over and cupped my face with his hand. 'No,' he said softly. 'I think it means there's something right with you.'

I smiled. 'The worst thing is that Duchovny just didn't care about Shelby,' I mused. 'I mean, she's his *daughter*. It's like . . . neither Sam nor Dad are my biological fathers, but I can't imagine them not paying a ransom for me. I mean, Sam kept looking for me for *years*.'

Jam shrugged. 'Not all fathers care about their children.'

I suddenly remembered the notches Jam had carved on the back of his DS. He'd once told me they represented the number of times he'd seen his own father in the past few years. Jam hadn't mentioned him for months.

'When did you last see *your* dad?' I asked.

'Months ago,' Jam said. 'Before last Christmas.' He disentangled himself from Madison. 'I'm going to walk around a bit. Warm up.'

It was obvious he didn't want to talk about his dad, but I was determined to try and find out how he felt about him.

'Jam?' I said as he stood up.

183

'Oh my God.' He was peering over the rock that we had sheltered behind, looking out towards the sea.

'What?' I left Madison on the sand and scrambled to my feet. My guts seemed to shrivel inside me as I followed Jam's gaze.

While we had been huddled behind the rock, the tide had been coming in. The closest waves were breaking just a few metres away.

Jam glanced round at me, his eyes wide with horror.

'The tide's coming in,' he breathed. 'The water is going to rise and rise.'

I looked round at the sheer sides of the cliff shooting up from the sand. Impossible to climb.

'And we can't get away,' I gasped. 'The sea's coming in – we're going to drown.'

25

Rising Tide

As the realisation that we were trapped in the bay sank in, it started to rain. I was so wet already that I barely noticed the first drops, but after a few seconds the drizzle turned harder and faster and within half a minute the water was pouring down, streaming off our clothes and down our backs.

Jam and I stood side by side, staring around the bay. The tide was rising fast. Only about fifty metres of cliff remained free from the water – and the sea was relentless, gaining ground along the beach with each new wave.

'There must be some way to climb up the cliffs,' I said.

Jam wiped the rain off his face. 'I told you already, I looked and there isn't.'

'I'm going to look again.' I set off around the bay. It was the middle of the night but the moon, gleaming between dark clouds, gave me just enough light to see.

I walked slowly, examining every inch of the rocks surrounding us. Jam was right. The cliff face was as smooth as if someone had been polishing it. There were a few ridges and potential footholds that might have made climbing possible if we'd had a rope and proper equipment, but we had nothing with us.

185

I crossed the beach back to Jam. *Jeez*, the place where we had sheltered was already under water. Jam had picked Madison up and was holding her in his arms, leaning against another stretch of rock.

'I can't see a way out of this.' His eyes were full of fear.

I stared back at him, my own panic suddenly rising. Jam had always been so solid . . . always made me feel there was hope.

'There has to be a way,' I insisted, forcing my anxiety down.

As I spoke, Madison stirred in Jam's arms.

'Lauren?' she said.

Jam set her down on the sand and she leaned against my side.

'What time is it, Lauren?' Madison yawned. 'When can we wave at the boats?'

I exchanged a look with Jam. The night sky was still pitch black. Which meant we must be at least a couple of hours away from the dawn. I looked around. The tide seemed to be rising faster and faster. Less than twenty square metres of beach remained visible.

'It's still very late,' I said. 'Or very, very early, depending on which way you look at it.'

Madison nodded seriously. 'I think this is the latest I've ever been up,' she said with a shiver. Her huge brown eyes widened as she looked up and took in the advancing waves. The water was now just a stone's throw away.

'The sea's got real close,' she said, sounding alarmed.

'We'll be fine.' I stroked her arm. 'You're doing good, babycakes.'

186

The rain was falling heavily now. I touched my hair. It was tangled from the salt of the sea and the wind.

'Guess we look like a pair of fright wigs, Mo,' I said, trying to smile.

'Well, you totally do.' She threw me a cheeky grin.

I looked up. *Jeez.* The waves were almost at our feet. I stared, mesmerised, at the water gushing up the sand, then sucking back.

What on earth were we going to do?

'Is that water going to reach us?' Madison's voice was suddenly uncertain.

'I think so,' I said.

Jam took off his belt. 'When it does, we're going to have to swim to stay up in the water,' he said. 'But we can keep together if we hold on to this.'

'Swim again?' Madison looked out at the sea. 'OK. Sure.'

She was trying to sound brave, but I could hear the terror in her voice. I was certain she was remembering how she nearly drowned in the sea beside Sonia Holtwood's boat. She had been reluctant to go in the water since – even swimming pools – and she wasn't a strong swimmer. She'd already had to battle against the current to make it onto this beach; how was she going to cope in the sea a second time?

'You won't have to swim much, Mo,' I said, trying to sound reassuring. 'Just kick your legs a bit. Jam and I will hold you up.'

A sudden, strong wave rushed up the beach and licked at

my toes. I stepped back, pressing myself against the smooth, chill rock behind.

Jam caught my eye. I knew that he was weighing up our chances. The odds were surely stacked against us. The sea was cold and the current was strong. We were already exhausted and hungry. Keeping ourselves afloat was going to be enough of a challenge, without having to help Madison survive the water.

'It'll be better than last time, Mo,' I said. 'I promise. That was the three of us too and we got through it.'

She nodded, but her chocolate-brown eyes glistened as she stared at the sea. Another wave lapped at my feet.

I looked out across the bay. I couldn't see the point where the sea met the sky. The darkness was terrifying.

'Maybe if we swim hard . . .' Jam said. 'Maybe we'll be able to get around the bay . . .'

I gulped, remembering my journey from Cooper's boat to the shore. That had been less than half the distance that we'd have to swim now – and I'd still had to fight to make it. Even without the fact that we'd be swimming against the tide *and* battling the current, there was no way we could survive a journey all the way round the cliffs.

I could see in Jam's face that he knew that too.

The water swirled around my ankles. My feet were so frozen already that the sea didn't feel particularly cold, but I knew that once we were properly immersed the chill would seep into our bones.

'We have to keep moving,' I said. 'Stay as warm as possible.'

'Right.' Jam jumped up and down. 'Yeah. Core temperature. Good thinking. Come on, Madison.'

Madison half-heartedly splashed in the water. Being shorter than me and Jam, it was almost up to her knees.

I closed my eyes. *Please, there must be a way through this.*

The water crept up my legs. Soon it would sweep my feet from under me. The others too. Then we would rise for a while, fighting the current and our own tiredness – before finally sinking.

Sinking under the water.

Unless . . .

I looked up. Rain attacked my skin like tiny knives, but I shielded my eyes with my hand and searched the rock far above our heads.

Yes. It was much bumpier and rougher up there . . . maybe uneven enough to provide handholds.

My heart beat faster as I thought it through. The sea was going to rise and we were going to rise with it. If we could manage to tread water and fight the current and stay close to the rock wall then maybe . . . just maybe . . . the water would lift us high enough to reach a ledge or some kind of foothold.

Maybe we could climb our way out of here after all.

'How high do you think the sea rises?' I turned to Jam, wiping the rain off my face.

'No idea.' His hair was plastered to his forehead.

I explained my idea.

'Let's hope you're right,' he said.

189

The water was up to our thighs now . . . up to Madison's waist. She was struggling to stay upright. I took Jam's belt and threaded it through Madison's jeans loops and my own. I fastened the buckle.

'We're tied together now,' I said. 'But you still have to move your arms and legs as much as possible to stay up in the water.'

Madison nodded. She was shivering again, her teeth chattering.

'Keep moving,' Jam ordered.

I kicked my legs under the water. The rain eased to a soft drizzle, then stopped.

'I can't touch the bottom any more,' Madison said anxiously.

'We'll be fine,' I repeated, hoping against hope it was true.

A few more minutes and the water cut my legs from under me. I was truly cold now – and bone weary, my limbs moving on adrenalin only.

The sea rose. There were still no lights out on the water, but the moon shrouded the bay in a misty glow. It was hard work staying close to the rock face. There was nothing to cling on to and the current kept dragging us away from the cliff and each other. I battled at the waves – one minute being sucked towards the sea, the next flung against the hard rock. Within minutes, I was bruised all over – and completely exhausted. Madison kicked and pulled at the water like we'd told her, but her movements were getting slower and slower and her weight was making it harder for me to keep myself afloat.

Water splashed against my chin. The wooden oval bobbed out in front of me. The salt stung my lips.

'Let's swim along the rock,' Jam gasped.

I nodded, following as he pulled himself through the water. Madison struggled to keep up with me. None of us were moving fast. I watched Jam just a few metres ahead. His strokes were slow and tired; like me he was having to fight hard against the current. Suddenly I felt overwhelmed with exhaustion. All I wanted to do was sleep. My arms and legs seemed to grow heavy. I closed my eyes, feeling Madison's weight dragging me lower into the water.

'Lauren!' Jam's yell echoed faintly across the bay. 'Look!'

My eyes sprang open. Madison was barely above water level. Her face was tipped back in the water: just her nose and tightly-shut eyes were visible. Jam was calling from about five metres away. He pointed up, towards the rock face above my head.

'What is that?' he yelled.

I followed his gaze to a vertical ridge in the rock face. The base of the ridge was an arm's length above my head. Even if I could reach it, it wouldn't provide a useful handhold.

'It's nothing.' I meant to shout the words, but they came out all hoarse. Salt water filled my mouth. *Ugh*. I coughed.

'No, look, Lauren.' Madison was open-eyed now, scrabbling in the water like a little puppy beside me.

I blinked. Stared harder at the ridge. And then I realised what the others had already seen.

The ridge was actually a narrow opening in the rock, about two metres high. I trod water, still staring upwards, while Jam swam back towards us.

'Must be a cave,' he gasped, reaching up his arm. His fingers just reached the bottom of the opening. It was only about thirty centimetres wide. Would that be big enough for us to crawl through?

'How far back d'you think it goes?' I said, trying to keep my mouth above the water. The waves were still pushing in, the sea rising.

'I can't see more than a metre inside,' Jam panted. 'But it's shelter.'

He was right. If we could just slip through the narrow opening at least we'd be safe from the tide, as long as it didn't go much higher.

'Worth a try,' I gasped.

The current was pulling us away from the cave. I forced my way back through the swirling water. Time passed. The sea rose. I was so tired now that I couldn't focus properly. Had it been one minute since we'd noticed the opening . . . or ten?

Madison had almost stopped moving. She was even lower in the water than before. Waves splashed at her nostrils. She spluttered, but clearly couldn't raise her head higher.

The sea was still rising. I reached up to the opening. I could hook my arm through the narrow gap now. With fumbling fingers, I undid the belt that linked me to Madison and tied her to Jam.

'Will you help me up?' I said. 'Then push Mo up to me?'

He nodded. 'Go.'

I hooked my arm through the opening. The rock was wet from the rain and difficult to grip, but I clung on as Jam made a stirrup with his hands under the water. I stepped into it, giving him my weight for a second.

With a roar, Jam shoved me upwards. I hauled and clawed my arm all the way into the opening, reaching for something to give me purchase. *There.* I found an edge on the rock and pulled my upper body sideways through the narrow gap. My ribs scraped painfully across the rock floor, but I was in. I dragged myself further into the cave. It widened . . . opened out. It was dark – I couldn't see how big it was, but there was room for me to twist round. Still on my side, I hauled my legs in after my body. I could barely feel them, but I struggled onto my knees and reached back through the opening.

I felt Madison's hand grasping for mine. I clutched her and pulled and she came slithering into the cave after me.

She gasped for breath. I lay her on the rocky ground. My eyes had adjusted to the darkness. I couldn't see where the cave ended, but I was certain it was big enough for the three of us to shelter in.

'We're going to be OK.' Hope rose inside me as I reached back through the opening for Jam. His hand met mine. I could see the surface of the sea beyond him. Still rising.

I pulled hard. One arm was through. His face appeared in the gap.

'Turn sideways,' I ordered.

Jam's eyes were screwed up with the effort of hauling himself up. He was trying to turn . . . to twist himself round so that he would fit through the opening. But his shoulders were too broad.

'It's no good,' he gasped. 'I can't get through.'

193

26
Through and Out

Jam forced both arms through the opening and twisted sideways. His shoulders were still too broad to pass.

'It's no good,' he said. 'I can't do it.'

Madison let out an agonised whimper beside me.

'Yes, you can.' I clutched Jam's wrist and braced myself against the side of the cave. I could feel the muscles in his forearm tighten.

'One, two, GO!' I yelled.

With a roar, he hauled himself forward. I pulled. He pushed. Both of us were yelling our heads off.

Again. He was almost through, his shoulders wedged tight against the sides of the opening. Again. A final effort and he squeezed through the entrance, the sharp rocks tearing through his shirt. He lay panting, on the ground.

Madison crawled over and the three of us clutched at each other.

'We're safe,' I said, needing to say the words out loud to make them feel real. 'We're going to be OK.'

My voice echoed round the cave. How big was this place? I stood up, my legs trembling, and felt round the walls. We seemed to be in an oval space in the rock, about three metres square.

'Lauren,' Madison said. 'I think the sea's coming in.'

I reached down and patted the floor of the cave. Water was trickling through, waves lapping at the opening we'd all just climbed through.

My stomach gave a sick lurch. If the sea was still rising then finding this hiding place didn't save us at all – it would flood and we would drown here.

'She's right,' I said, trying to hold in the terrible feeling of panic that swirled in my guts.

'That's not good,' Jam muttered. He was on his feet, feeling round the walls too. I could make out his shadow, moving across the floor.

Madison scuttled over beside me. 'Will the water fill this cave up?' she said.

'I don't know. It depends how much further in the tide comes and how far back the cave goes.'

'Why don't we walk through there?' Madison pointed to the darkest part of the cave, where the wall dipped towards a jagged archway.

It was a tunnel. Not a man-made concrete tunnel like the one under the beach hut at Norbourne promenade, but a narrow, rocky crevice – like a split running through the heart of the rock.

Jam and I rushed over.

'That is awesome, Mo.' I reached down and hugged her. 'You're a star for finding it.'

Madison beamed.

'Let's see where it goes,' Jam said.

He set off first, Madison behind him and me bringing up the rear. There was only room for us to walk single file and Jam and I both had to stoop. The tunnel was very uneven. The walls grew narrower, then wider, and the ceiling was low for ages, then suddenly opened out.

It felt like we walked for miles, but maybe I was just scared and exhausted. Stumbling through a tunnel in the dark, where you can't see your hand in front of your face and you don't know where you're going, isn't easy – and when you're tired and cold, every step seems to take forever.

As we walked on, a breeze blew down the tunnel towards us.

'That's a good sign,' Jam said. 'We must be heading outside.'

We kept going. Madison tripped frequently and I was so tired I could barely place one foot in front of the other. But the wind coming through the tunnel grew stronger and cooler, encouraging us on.

At last the tunnel lightened.

'I can see a way out,' Jam exclaimed.

We hurried on and a couple of minutes later we emerged onto the slope of a high cliff, surrounded by other higher cliffs. It was dawn at last and the sky was a swirl of misty blues and pinks and oranges, with the sea just visible in the distance. We scrambled away from it, over the rocks. After a few minutes' hard climbing, we found ourselves overlooking a large, but empty car park on the edge of a town. It didn't look like Norbourne, but the buildings were similar in size and design. The car park itself was deserted but traffic zoomed along the road beyond.

We made our way down to the car park. Jam went over to the sign to see where we were. We were all exhausted, and shivering from cold. Madison's hair was stuck to her face and she had a graze on her cheek. Jam's shirt was ripped to pieces. And yet, in that moment, I felt euphoric.

'We've done it.' My heart raced with relief. Black smudges appeared at the edges of my vision. I felt light-headed . . . giddy.

Madison looked up at me, her huge brown eyes soft and solemn.

'What about Shelby?' she said. 'What about—?'

But I didn't hear the rest of what she said because the black smudges were spreading and filling me up and my head whirled and my legs buckled underneath me.

I woke from the blackness to warm, dry sheets and the distant smell of coffee. A small body was squeezed up close to mine. I opened my eyes. Madison was curled up beside me on the bed.

Was I at home?

No. It was a hospital room – we were on one of those trolleys, a curtain drawn all round the bed. An IV was hooked into the back of my hand. I sat up, feeling drained. A jug of water stood beside the bed, but I was no longer desperately thirsty.

I glanced down at the plaster covering the place where the IV fluids entered my hand. I was seriously contemplating yanking it out so that I could get off the bed and see exactly where I was, when the curtains opened and Annie appeared, a polystyrene cup of steaming coffee in her hand. Her face creased with relief as she took in the fact that I was awake.

'Oh, Lauren,' she said. Annie's eyes were red and sore-looking and her skin drawn and grey. Misery was etched into her face, yet she attempted a weak smile. 'How are you feeling?'

'I'm OK,' I said.

'Are you sure?' Annie said anxiously. 'They examined you . . . said you were just suffering from exhaustion and that you were a bit dehydrated.'

I nodded, touched my side where I'd scraped it across the rock. A little tender, but no more than a graze.

'Where's Jam?' I said.

'He's on the phone to his mother,' Annie said. 'I've called your mom and dad. They're getting the next flight home.'

'Oh.' I sat back against the wall behind me, adjusting to this news. If Mum and Dad were cutting short their holiday to come back to see me then they must be really worried about me. Which meant a lot of fuss though, if I was honest, I was glad they were on their way. 'What's the time? When will they get here?'

Annie consulted her watch. 'It's 4 pm. They'll be here by tomorrow morning and they're coming straight down to the holiday home to pick you up.'

'Right.' I frowned. Surely the sun had only just been rising when we'd made our way out of the cave? 'Is it really four o'clock?'

198

Annie nodded. 'You fainted just before some passers-by turned up. They called for an ambulance. Jam said you woke up for a second, then you went straight to sleep. Madison insisted on staying with you.' We both looked at Madison, who was breathing deeply and evenly beside me. Annie hesitated. 'Shelby's still missing.'

I stared at her, suddenly remembering everything that had happened yesterday.

Annie looked me in the eye. 'Jam told me what happened . . . how Rick was behind the kidnapping and . . .' She tailed off.

'Sam's letters?' I asked.

Annie looked away and lowered her voice. 'I never wanted you girls to know about *any* of that,' she said.

I didn't know what to say. I still felt numb when I thought about my own biological father being some anonymous sperm donor. After all, Dad was Dad and Sam was the man who'd originally fathered me . . . there wasn't room in my brain for anyone else.

As for Shelby, it was just too embarrassing to imagine Annie having an affair with that horrible Duchovny.

Thinking of Duchovny brought me back to Cooper and how he'd rescued me on that cliff top.

'Did Jam tell you what Cooper did to Rick and the other kidnappers?' I shivered as I remembered the sound of the bodies falling from the cliff.

'Yes.' Annie twisted her hands together. 'And I know it means Shelby's in terrible danger too . . .'

199

'Are the police looking for her?'

'Yes, but they have no idea where Cooper is renting this house of his.'

At that moment Jam came in, swiftly followed by a doctor who examined me. As the doctor removed my IV and checked me over, Madison woke up. After that, Annie bought us all sandwiches from the canteen and a police officer came to interview me. I told him everything I knew – including how I'd stolen the painting from Duchovny's house. The man nodded and grunted and took a few notes, but he couldn't – or wouldn't – answer any of my questions.

It was soon clear to me that, as Annie had said, the police had absolutely no idea where Cooper was keeping Shelby. Or why.

It was 7 pm and a light drizzle was falling when we got back to the holiday home. Two police officers drove us home. They helped us inside, then went back to their car where they were going to stay, keeping watch over us, all night.

Madison hadn't left my side all day, but once we got indoors, Annie insisted on taking her up to bed.

'Come on, Madison,' she said firmly. 'You can't stop yawning.'

'Can Lauren read me a story first?' Madison pleaded.

Annie rolled her eyes. 'Not tonight. Come on.'

'Night, Mo.' I gave her a hug and watched her follow Annie up the stairs.

I heated up some soup and Jam and I sat at the kitchen table. We didn't say much. I knew that Carla, Jam's mum, was on her way down here to pick him up. Jam had said she was angry with him for running off to be with me.

'D'you think she'll try and stop us seeing each other?' I said.

'It doesn't matter what my mum says,' he said, leaning closer to me. 'Nobody will ever be able to stop me from seeing you.'

I closed my eyes and we kissed.

As we drew apart, I cleared my throat. It was scary to speak my feelings out loud, but I knew I had to say this:

'Thank you for . . . for everything,' I said. 'It made all the difference you . . . you being here with me . . .'

Jam tilted his head to one side. His expression was simultaneously exasperated and tender.

'I know,' he said.

I grinned.

At that moment, the phone inside Annie's bag started ringing.

'D'you think that's your mum or mine?' I said, reaching into the bag.

'Your mum's on an aeroplane.' Jam frowned. 'So I guess it's mine.'

I took out the mobile. The number was flashing up on the screen. Jam peered at the phone.

'That's not Mum's number,' he said.

For a second I wondered if it could be Cooper Trent. I shivered.

I glanced towards the door. Annie was still upstairs. It was highly likely she'd fallen asleep next to Madison. I didn't want to disturb them. 'It's probably just one of Annie's friends.' I lifted the phone to my ear. 'Hello?'

'Lauren?' It was Shelby, her voice cracking as she spoke. 'Listen, you have to get everyone out of the house. Cooper knows you're alive and he's on his way to kill you all now.'

27

Carter's of Norbourne

I froze. 'Shelby?' I gasped. 'Where are you? What—?'

'There's no time,' Shelby insisted, her voice rising shrilly. 'Cooper saw a news report that you and the others were alive. He's *coming* for you. Keep Mom's phone. I'll call you again in a minute. Just get out of the house.' She rang off.

I put Annie's phone down on the kitchen table. My head was spinning. I knew I had to act . . . and act fast, but I couldn't think straight.

'What is it, Lauren?' Jam demanded.

I repeated what Shelby had said. My voice felt somehow disconnected to the rest of me. Despite the need for the police officers stationed outside, I'd assumed the worst was over – that even if Cooper found out we'd escaped he wouldn't risk approaching us . . . that Shelby would be found . . .

'We have to get Annie and Madison,' I went on, forcing myself to pull it together. 'We have to go outside to the police car.'

I said the words, but I didn't move.

Jam rushed out of the room. I could hear him pounding up the stairs, yelling Annie's name.

The phone rang again. The same number.

'Shelby?' I said.

'Are you out?' she said.

'Almost. How did you get away from Cooper?'

'He drove to Norbourne. Left me locked up in his car. I got out . . . ran up this road . . . broke in here to use the phone. But I've hurt my ankle. I can't walk. Are you out now?'

'In a sec.'

'Hurry!' She ended the call.

I shoved Annie's mobile in her bag, slung the bag over my shoulder and rushed into the hallway. Annie was on the bottom step of the stairs, Jam just behind her with Madison, fast asleep, in his arms.

'What's going on, Lauren?' Annie was trembling, her hands twisting round each other.

The sight of her anxiety somehow calmed me down. Someone had to be strong.

'Outside.' I pointed to the front door.

She ran over, her fingers fumbling, flailing at the catch.

I pushed her hand away and opened the door. The night air was cool and smelled of rain. It was still drizzling. Annie stumbled outside. I held the door open for Jam. We raced along the path and onto the pavement. I pointed at the police car parked opposite. The officers inside would help us.

'Over there!' I said.

Annie sped off. As I followed her across the road, her phone – still in her bag over my shoulder – rang again.

'Lauren?' Shelby sounded more frightened than before. 'Are you out of the house now?'

'Yes.' I glanced up and down the road. There was no-one about . . . no sign of Cooper Trent. 'He's not here yet.'

'OK, good.'

'Where are you?' I asked.

Shelby hesitated. 'Carter's of Norbourne. It's an office building. There's a map here and I'm seriously like only a couple of minutes away from the holiday home . . . The stores at the end of our road lead down to the top of this one . . . it should be the first turning on the left. My ankle's really bad. Er . . . can you send the police to pick me up?'

'We're with the police right n—'

Annie's scream filled the air, stopping me mid-word. I spun round. I couldn't see what had happened at first. Annie was in the way. She staggered backwards, her hand over her mouth.

'Is that Mom?' Shelby shrieked into my ear.

'Oh, no!' Jam said beside me.

I looked across the road and into the police car opposite.

Everything inside me seemed to shrink and crumple.

Both officers were unconscious, their heads lolling on their chests.

'He's here,' Annie screamed. 'Oh my God, Cooper's already *here*!'

I met Jam's eyes for a second, then looked up and down the street again. There was no-one around.

'Call the police,' Annie was still shrieking.

'Wait,' I said. 'Where's *your* car, Annie?'

Annie looked wildly up and down the road. 'There.' She pointed at the hire car. 'But I don't think I can drive.'

'You have to,' I said, fishing for the keys in Annie's bag which was still over my shoulder. 'Cooper's obviously already here . . . he must have gone round the back of the house to break in. We have to get away before he realises we're not inside.'

'Oh God, oh God, oh God.' Annie ran over to her car.

I followed, holding Annie's phone while searching for the car keys in her bag. Shelby was still on the other end of the line. She could presumably hear what was happening, but there was no time to talk to her. I *had* to find those car keys.

There. I yanked them out of the bag and unlocked the car.

Annie's fingers shook as she opened the driver seat door. 'I can't do this,' she muttered. 'It's too much.'

'Yes, you *can*,' I urged.

Jam got in the back with Madison. I sat by Annie at the front.

She fitted the key into the ignition. The engine revved.

'Let me speak to Shelby,' she said.

'There's no time,' I protested.

'I want to talk to her.'

I handed Annie the phone, then glanced anxiously round. There was still no sign of anyone on the street – but I knew how fast Cooper could move. He could be here already, in the shadows, just seconds away.

'Hello, Shelby?' Annie turned to me. 'She's not there.'

I put the phone to my ear. It was true. The line was still open, but Shelby was no longer on the other end.

'Dial 999,' Jam said.

I tried to end the call, but the phone wouldn't let me. 'Something's stopping me from making a new call,' I said.

'But it's the only phone we've got with us,' Jam said desperately.

A dark figure appeared at the end of the street. A man. He was walking briskly towards the car.

'Drive!' I shouted.

Annie screeched onto the road.

'Where's Shelby?' she sobbed, the car veering wildly across the central line. 'What's happened to her?'

'She's in Norbourne,' I said. 'She said she'd hurt her ankle so she couldn't walk.'

'Oh God,' Annie moaned.

The car reached the top of the road. The shops Shelby had mentioned appeared on the right. I pointed to them. 'She said she was in a building just past these shops . . . first turning on the left.'

'OK.' Annie clutched the steering wheel tighter. Without signalling, she swung the car onto the road with the shops, cutting in front of an estate car. It honked its horn angrily, but Annie didn't seem to notice.

'Down there.' I pointed to the road coming up on the left.

'Wait,' Jam said. 'We should drive to the police station. Or stop and ask someone to use their phone.'

'Shelby first,' Annie insisted.

'She's hurt, Jam,' I said. 'She can't walk.'

The office building Shelby had described was already visible. A sign reading *Carter's of Norbourne* stood at the front.

'Where is she?' Annie pulled over, leaving half the car sticking out into the road.

She opened her door and got out. 'Shelby?' she yelled.

'Mom!' Shelby's answer came from inside the building, her voice a mix of terror and relief. 'Mom, is that you?'

I looked up. Shelby was silhouetted in a first-floor window. It was the only room in the building with the light on. Annie ran over.

I held the mobile up to my ear again, but there was still no sound from the other end. Why hadn't Shelby hung the phone up properly?

'I hurt myself, Mom,' Shelby was sobbing as she called out from the window. 'I can't walk.'

'I'm coming,' Annie yelled back.

'Annie's going to need help if Shelby can't walk,' I said to Jam. 'Stay here with Madison.'

'No way,' Jam said, laying Madison gently down on the back seat. 'I'll come with you. We can call the police from inside the building.'

Jam and I got out of the car and joined Annie at the front door. I glanced over my shoulder at Madison. I didn't like leaving her, not after everything that had happened, not even while she was within eyesight.

'I can't see a way in.' Annie was breathless with agitation, almost hopping up and down on the spot.

Jam pointed to the broken window to the right of the door. 'That must be how Shelby got in.'

Annie nodded. She glanced back at the car, wringing her hands. 'Is Madison still asleep?'

'Yes,' I said.

'I don't want her to wake up and us not be there.' Annie clutched at her hair. She looked over at the broken window, desperation in her eyes. I could see she was torn between going after one daughter and protecting another.

'You're right, you shouldn't leave Mo,' I said firmly. 'Jam and I will go in and get Shelby. You wait here with your phone . . . see if it starts working again. You can keep an eye on Madison *and* call the police.'

'OK,' Annie gulped. 'Be careful.'

Jam was already half through the window.

I scrambled after him, feeling the uneven crunch of the glass on the carpet at my feet. We were in some kind of storage room. We raced out into a hallway. The stairs up to the first floor were straight ahead of us.

Jam sped up them, two steps at a time.

'Shelby?' I yelled. 'We're coming.'

We reached the landing. The room at the front with the light on was on the left. That was, surely, where Shelby had called out to us.

'Shelby?' Jam said, walking in through the door.

I joined him in the office room. A row of desks, complete

with computers and phones, met my eyes. Piles of paper littered the floor. Blinds hung at the window. Two filing cabinets stood at either end of the far wall, a shelf groaning with box files running between them.

'Shelby?' My voice echoed Jam's.

But Shelby was not in the room.

28

The Accident

'Where's Shelby gone?' I said. 'She said she couldn't walk.'

Jam pointed across the office to the desk by the window. A phone receiver lay off the hook, on its side beside the landline phone base.

'D'you think that's the phone she used?' he whispered.

I scuttled over and picked up the receiver. The office building suddenly felt creepily quiet.

'Annie?' I said quietly.

No reply.

'If that was the phone Shelby used then Annie should still be on the other end of the line, shouldn't she?' Jam said.

I tiptoed to the window and peered outside. Annie's car was still parked in the road. I couldn't see inside to check if Madison was still lying across the back seat, but there was definitely no sign of Annie herself either near the car or by the front door where we had left her.

'I can't see her,' I said.

'Man, this is all really weird,' Jam whispered, looking around the room. 'Even if Shelby somehow managed to drag herself out of here why would she go? *Where* would she go? This is the only room with a light on.'

I gulped. 'Let's just dial 999,' I said. 'This place is totally freaking me out.' I replaced the handset.

'Help!' Shelby's shriek made me jump. Her voice came from the floor above us.

Jam gripped my arm. 'She's upstairs,' he breathed.

'Lauren?' Shelby shouted. 'Is that you?'

I rushed out of the office, Jam at my side. We raced up the stairs to the second floor. Several doors led off from a small landing.

'Shelby?' Jam shouted.

'In here!' Her voice came from one of the rooms on the right.

We darted inside.

The room was lit only by the moonlight that shone through a tiny dormer window. A storage space, far messier than the one on the ground floor, with filing cabinets lining the walls and a long chest of drawers under the window.

It took me a moment to spot Shelby. She was lying on the ground, hunched over beside one of the filing cabinets. She gazed up at us. Her face was white and tear-streaked. 'I'm sorry,' she said.

'Why are you—?' As I spoke, the door to the room slammed shut. A key twisted in the lock. 'Hey!' I spun round and yanked at the handle. The door wouldn't open. 'Hey! Let us out!'

There was silence outside in the small hallway. Then the sound of footsteps, pattering down the stairs.

I turned back to Shelby. 'Who's out there?' I said, feeling desperate. 'What's going on?'

Beside me, Jam hurled himself at the door. It shuddered, but the lock didn't break. 'Oy!' he yelled.

'Shelby?' I marched over to her.

She was staring at the thin grey carpet beneath her.

Wham. Jam barged the door again. It held.

'Shelby, what the hell is happening here?' My voice shook with emotion. My head was spinning. Fury filled me and I opened my mouth to yell.

But at that moment, Shelby looked up and I saw the red mark on her cheek and the thin metal chain that ran from her wrist to the filing cabinet she was leaning against.

Shocked, I sank to my knees. 'Shelby?' I stared at the chain. I couldn't make sense of it. She'd been on the phone to us just minutes ago. How had she ended up here, in this storage room where – I looked quickly round – there were no phones?

Jam gave up on the door and strode over. His mouth fell open as he took in Shelby's chain.

'Did Cooper Trent do that?' he asked.

Shelby nodded. Her lower lip trembled. 'He made me call out to you downstairs, then he brought me up here and tied me up.'

I stared at her in horror. 'You mean he's *trapped* us here?' I said.

Shelby nodded.

Jam raced to the dormer window. He pushed at the glass, but it would only open a fraction.

'Hey!' he shouted through the crack. 'Help!'

I turned to Shelby. 'But . . . but you said Cooper Trent was going to the holiday house,' I said. 'And he *did*. I saw the police officers he knocked out.'

'Cooper went there earlier,' Shelby explained shakily. 'He brought me here, went to deal with the police officers outside the holiday house, then came back and made me ring you. He jammed the call too, so you couldn't use the phone again. It all happened real fast.'

'Help!' Jam shouted through the dormer window again. He turned to me. 'I can't hear anyone outside.'

'But Annie's there.' I jumped up. 'What's Cooper done with her?' I said to Shelby. 'What about Madison?'

'I don't know.' Shelby's mouth trembled.

I sank back down to the ground beside her. There was a short, tense silence.

'I don't get any of this, Shelby,' Jam said gently. 'Go back to the beginning. Why didn't Cooper dump you in the bay like the rest of us?'

Shelby fought back her tears. 'He still thought he could get a ransom from that man . . . my . . . Duchovny.' Shelby sniffed. 'But before Cooper could approach him again, Duchovny turned up . . . he must have followed Cooper home.' She looked up at me. 'Duchovny came for one thing,' she said. 'To get that painting back that you stole.'

I met Shelby's gaze. The thought that she was only half expressing rang as clearly in my head as if she'd said it out loud.

He came for the painting, not to rescue me.

214

A confusion of emotions welled up inside me. I couldn't look at her. I gave the chain tied to her wrist a tug. It was firmly fastened to the back of the filing cabinet. Unbreakable without proper tools.

'I thought the painting wasn't worth that much,' Jam said, looking confused.

'Apparently it was worth millions,' Shelby said. 'Anyway, they . . . there was a fight.'

'What happened?' I asked.

Shelby leaned against the filing cabinet. She closed her eyes and sighed. 'Duchovny was hurt, but he got away with the painting. Cooper brought me and the money here.'

'So you didn't escape from him?' Jam said.

Shelby shook her head.

I frowned. 'I don't understand. Why did he bring you here?'

'So that I'd be away from his house when the police track him down and . . .' Shelby's face pinked, 'and so that I could make sure you two came here.'

'Us?' Jam said.

Shelby nodded. 'Cooper found out you were still alive. He knew you'd be able to identify him and he knows that if the police get him they'll need our testimony to convict him,' she explained. 'Once he knew you'd escaped from the bay, he came up with this plan to trap you here. I was just the bait.'

I sat back on my heels. It was an ingenious plan. And, so far, I had to admit that it had worked. But why? I looked round at the empty storage room. What possible reason could Cooper have for locking us into this office building?

'What's he going to do with us?' Jam said, echoing my thoughts.

'And what about Annie and Madison?' I said, thinking again about how I hadn't been able to see Annie outside.

'I don't know,' Shelby said.

I stood up, my heart beating fast. 'We have to get out of here . . . make sure the others are OK.'

I crossed the room and tried the door again. It was still locked fast. The only other way out was through the tiny dormer window that Jam had managed to open a few centimetres. I went over and pushed at it myself. It didn't open any further, but the night air rushed through – cool and damp on my face and carrying the faint tang of salt from the sea.

'We won't get through here,' I said.

Shelby held up her chained arm. 'Well, I certainly won't.' She attempted a grin. 'Or are you saying I'm fat?'

It took me a second to realise she was joking. Black humour was the last thing I'd expected.

'Yeah, Shelbs.' I forced a smile back. 'You're a hog.'

She smiled ruefully at me and it occurred to me how bizarre it was that these terrifying circumstances marked the first time, ever, that Shelby had made any attempt to be friendly with me.

Jam cleared his throat. 'Er . . . Lauren? Shelby?' He was standing beside the door that led out to the tiny second-floor hallway. 'Look.' He pointed to the base of the door.

I frowned, trying to work out what on earth he was staring at.

And then I saw it.

Smoke. Grey-white and wisp-faint, it curled under the door. Jam bent down and sniffed at the gap between the door and the floor.

'What's that?' Shelby's voice quavered.

Jam looked up at me and the terrified look in his eyes told me the truth before my brain had even processed what the smoke meant.

'Cooper's set the building on fire,' I said.

29

In Chains

Shelby gasped. 'Fire?' she said.

Jam nodded. 'That's why he lured us here . . . so he could kill us and make it look like an accident.'

'No-one's going to believe this was an accident,' I insisted, rushing over to the door as another wisp of smoke blew underneath it and into the room. 'I mean surely this smoke should be setting off an alarm . . . which means Cooper must have disabled the system.'

'It doesn't matter,' Jam said. 'Even if Cooper set the fire and stopped the alarms from going off there won't be any proof it was *him* who did it.'

'Just as without our evidence against him, there won't be any proof that he stole the two million or kidnapped us to try and get more money out of Duchovny,' Shelby said.

'We *have* to break this door down,' I said, squaring up to it.

Jam looked doubtful, but he stood beside me. Across the room, Shelby struggled to her feet. The chain that bound her to the filing cabinet was only a metre or so long – there was no way she could make it to the door.

'Don't worry, Shelby, Annie's outside. She'll call the fire brigade,' Jam said.

He met my eyes. I could see he knew as well as I did that it was highly likely Cooper had already got to Annie . . . that there was no-one else who knew we were here . . . no-one to save us . . .

My guts twisted into a knot.

'Plus, there must be a phone in the next room,' Jam went on, reassuringly.

'Yes,' I added. 'If we can get out of here we can call the fire brigade ourselves.'

I half expected Shelby to freak out about being chained up . . . to start shrieking that she was scared . . . but she said nothing, just offered me a curt nod then looked at the door.

'Go on,' she said. 'Try and break it down.'

On a count of three, Jam and I hurled ourselves at the door. The lock held.

'Again,' I said.

The door shook, but it still didn't open.

'Let's ram something heavy against it,' Jam suggested.

I looked round for something that was heavy enough to break down the door, but that we could manage to lift.

'Here,' Jam called from across the room. 'Help me with this, Lauren.'

He was lifting one side of a small filing cabinet. I rushed over and took hold of the other side. It was heavy. My arms strained with the effort of raising it.

Grey smoke was curling under the door. As we positioned ourselves, ready to ram the lock, Jam coughed.

'We need something over our mouths,' I said.

'In a minute.' Jam steeled himself. 'Ready?'

I nodded.

'Go!'

We charged at the door, forcing the bulky cabinet against the wood. A huge dent appeared beside the lock.

'Again!' Jam ordered.

Again we rammed the cabinet against the door. Another dent. We were both coughing now. Smoke was still seeping into the room – grey and acrid.

'Again!'

This time the wood around the lock splintered. We set down the cabinet and Jam shouldered the door.

It flew open. Smoke billowed into the room. I turned away, choking, my eyes watering. I ripped off my jumper and held it over my mouth, but the smoke seemed to fill my lungs like acid vapour, stripping away at my throat. I was bent double, coughing like my insides were going to come right out of my mouth. At last I managed to stop. I looked up. Shelby was hunched against the wall, coughing into her cardigan which was stuffed over her mouth. She stared at me over the top of the material, her eyes wide and terrified.

Jam was nowhere to be seen.

I darted out onto the landing and nearly collided with him.

'No phones up here,' he panted. 'I'm gonna go back to that one downstairs.'

I watched him race down the steps. The smoke here was steady, but not dense. I couldn't see any flames or feel any heat, though the smell of burning plastic filled the air. It didn't matter. I knew that the smoke was every bit as dangerous as the fire. More, perhaps. If we breathed in too many noxious fumes we would collapse long before the flames themselves reached us.

I took a step after Jam. I wanted to follow him . . . to run down the stairs and out of the building. But what about Shelby? She was stuck here. I glanced over my shoulder. She was still hunched in the corner, coughing into her cardigan.

I took another step away, then stopped again.

The argument raged in my head. Shelby didn't care about me. I needed to get out of here for the sake of the people who did . . . Jam and Madison and Mum and Dad and Rory . . . even Annie.

As I hesitated, a cloud of thick smoke rolled up the stairs towards me. Choking, I staggered backwards, my sore eyes squeezed tight shut against the sting of the fumes. The landing suddenly filled with heat. I forced my eyes open. From being relatively clear a few seconds ago, the staircase below me was now engulfed in flames. Panic seized me.

'Jam!' I yelled. 'JAM!'

'I'm here.' Jam's voice rose up towards me through the fire.

He had made it down to the first floor. I caught a glimpse of his profile through the smoke which whirled, dirty and thick, all around him. The fire hissed and crackled up the stairs.

'Can you get to the ground floor?' I shouted.

'Yes.' Jam hesitated. He turned and looked up at me. 'But what about you and Shelby?'

I gazed down at him, my eyes watering from the smoke that whirled around me.

The staircase between the second and first floors was now impassable.

There was no way down for me and Shelby. I could see in Jam's face that he knew this – but he didn't want to leave me.

'Go on,' I insisted. 'We'll be fine. We'll find another way.'

Without waiting for his reply, I turned away and darted across the landing. In addition to the storage room, where we'd left Shelby, there were three other rooms. I opened each door in turn. One, the nearest to the stairs, was empty save for a stack of chairs and some ancient-looking computers piled in one corner. It contained no windows and was already filled with smoke. I left it and moved to the next room.

A bathroom. Tiny, also with no window. There was less smoke in here, for some reason.

I ran the water in the sink, holding my jumper under the tap until it was damp. As I put it up to my face, water ran down my neck, but it was definitely easier to breathe.

Clutching the sodden top over my mouth I opened the door to the fourth and final room, praying that I would find a proper window inside.

There was hardly any smoke here yet. I shut the door behind me and looked round. I was in another storage room complete with more filing cabinets, and piles of paper. A single dormer window was set into the sloping roof. Unfortunately it was, if anything, smaller than the one in the other room. I rushed over and pushed it open. A rush of cold night air – and the smell of burning – filled my nostrils.

At least it opened more than a few centimetres. I dragged a chair beneath the window and shoved my head through. The roof below slid away at a dizzying angle. There was no way I could stand on this roof, but the opening did offer some relief from the smoke. My heart leaped. If I stayed here I would be able to breathe clean air until the fire fighters arrived.

And then I remembered Shelby.

I hesitated for a second, then turned and went back onto the landing. The fire was at the top of the stairs, flames starting to lick across the carpet. I raced through the smoke and into the room where Shelby lay. She was still coughing badly, her cardigan covering her face.

I ran over and grabbed her shoulder. She looked up at me, her red-rimmed eyes registering shock.

'Lauren, I thought you'd gone,' she said.

I took the jumper away from my mouth.

'There's no way downstairs,' I said. Acrid smoke burned the back of my throat and I coughed. 'But there's another room where there's less smoke.'

Shelby held up her wrist, still attached by the chain to the filing cabinet. 'I can't move.' Her voice was strangely flat and calm.

'We'll sort that.' I brought the jumper back up to my mouth and took in a shallow breath. I was starting to feel light-headed. How long did we have before we passed out from the toxic fumes?

Trying not to think about it, I examined the chain round Shelby's wrist. It was securely and tightly fastened. The skin below it was red raw where she had obviously tried to slide it over her hand. Clearly there was no point trying to do that again. I felt along the chain to the point where it was fastened to the filing cabinet. It was threaded through a loop of metal at the cabinet base, then disappeared between the cabinet and the wall.

'We need to move this out of the way,' I said.

Shelby turned round and, together, we wrenched the cabinet a few centimetres away from the wall. I bent down, my lungs stinging and my eyes watering. Trying to breathe as shallowly as possible, I peered at the chain. It had been wound through the bars of the air duct grille that was set into the base of the wall. I felt through to the end of the chain. It was padlocked.

I sat back, my heart pounding, fighting the dizziness that filled my head.

'Can you get it free, Lauren?' Shelby sounded terrified.

'Yes.' I nodded for emphasis, but the truth was I couldn't possibly see how I could get the chain out of the grille.

The chain was too strong and the padlock too sturdy to break. Maybe if I'd had half an hour and an axe I might have done it.

But I had neither.

I stared at the grille. Well, maybe if I couldn't get the chain out of the grille I could just get the grille out of the wall.

I gripped both ends of the chain and gave the whole thing a yank.

Nothing happened.

'Here.' Shelby shuffled back to give me more space. 'Use the wall to push against.'

I propped myself against the filing cabinet and pressed my feet to the wall above the grille.

I pulled hard on the chain.

Still no movement.

Shelby swore, her voice rising in panic. 'Oh my God, Lauren.'

'We're going to do this,' I insisted.

I got up. Holding my sodden jumper to my mouth I raced across the room. There had to be something here that would help me remove the grille.

I yanked open the top drawer of the row of drawers that ran along the far wall. It was full of stationery. I flung it onto the floor, then moved onto the next. It was full of scraps of string and tacks and nails and rubber bands. I threw it onto the floor beside the first.

'See if there's anything there we can use,' I said, shoving both drawers closer to Shelby.

She bent over, still coughing into her cardigan, sorting through the contents.

I went back to the chest of drawers: there were blocks of A4 paper, bundles of envelopes, boxes of staples . . .

'Come *on*,' I muttered to myself.

The room was thick with smoke now. My eyes were stinging. I tried to take tiny, shallow breaths. Panicky thoughts sped through my head. How long had the fire been raging?

Was Jam OK? I strained my ears, hoping to hear the *nee naw* of a fire engine's siren. But I could hear nothing over the hiss of the fire and the soft thuds on the floor behind me, as Shelby ransacked the drawers I'd given her.

'What about this?' she said.

I spun round. Shelby was holding up a small metal ruler. We both glanced over at the grille behind the filing cabinet. It was held in place by two screws, one at either end.

Another burst of smoke filled the room. I bent double, eyes squeezed tight shut. I was coughing so badly it felt like my lungs were about to explode out of my throat.

I forced my eyes open. 'Let's try it,' I said, snatching the ruler off her.

There was just enough room for me to fit the tip of the metal bar into the first screw on the grille. As I steadied it, black smudges gathered at the edges of my vision.

No. I felt horribly giddy, like I had done when we'd got free from the cave earlier.

I turned the tiny ruler, focusing everything I had on making sure it didn't slip out of the screw. I reckoned I had less than a minute before I blacked out from the smoke.

This was our only chance.

30

The Burning

I twisted the ruler again. The screw was now jutting out from the grille.

'It's working,' I said.

'Good,' Shelby croaked.

Another twist and the first screw fell onto the floor. With trembling fingers, I set to work on the second screw. Around me the smoke was growing thicker. I narrowed my eyes, trying in vain to minimise the amount of smoke getting into them. They stung badly.

I concentrated on turning the screwdriver. I was so dizzy I could barely keep myself upright, but I kept going. Another twist. Another. I lost all sense of time. All my focus was on this screw and this metal ruler and this moment.

At last the screw fell out. *Yes*. Hope surged through me.

I gripped the chain threaded through the bars of the grille and yanked hard. With a sucking noise, the grille came away from its setting.

'Look!' I held up the grille and turned to show Shelby.

But her eyes were closed. She was lying, slumped on the floor. The cardigan which she had been clutching to her mouth lay on the ground beside her.

Had she passed out from the smoke?

I scrambled over. 'Wake up, Shelby!'

Her head lolled on her chest. I said her name again. No response. I reached back my hand and slapped her hard on the cheek.

'Aagh!' It came out as a low moan, but her eyelids flickered. She coughed.

I shook her shoulders. 'Get up!' I ordered.

Eyes still closed, Shelby stirred. She reached out her arms and I helped her to stand. I could barely stay upright myself. My head was spinning, my throat clogged with smoke.

'Come *on*!' I tried to yell, but all that came out was a hoarse rasp.

'OK,' Shelby muttered.

Leaning against me, she shuffled forward. I pushed open the door to the hallway. A wall of heat and smoke smacked us in the face. Flames were spreading across the landing. We both turned away, coughing violently. I could feel Shelby slipping down my side and gripped her more tightly.

Come on, come on.

The dizziness in my head was building. Black smudges floated across my vision. We only had seconds to get to the relative safety of the second storage room before the smoke and the fire overwhelmed us. I pushed myself on, keeping tight hold of Shelby. She was moaning now, dragging herself across the floor. Another step and we'd reach that back room. Just one more, just one more.

There. I pushed the door open and flung Shelby inside. She staggered across the room, collapsing in a heap at the base of the chair under the open dormer window. I slammed the door shut. The air was smoky in here, but nowhere near to the same extent as on the landing, or in the room we had just left.

I followed Shelby over to the window, clambered onto the chair so my head was outside and took a few deep breaths of the cold night air. The black smudges at the edges of my vision smoothed away.

I could see nothing except the roof tiles and the dark sky above – and hear nothing except the crackle of the fire. The smell of burning drifted up towards me. I tried to shout 'help!' but my throat was too sore. All that came out was a useless gasp.

I got down off the chair, feeling dizzy from the exertion of attempting to shout. I leaned against the wall, trying to work out what we needed to do next.

Smoke was still slipping through, round the sides and at the base of the door, but the fresh air from the dormer window would buy us a little time. And, surely, even if Jam or Annie hadn't been able to call for help *someone* would have seen the fire by now. Hope rose inside me. All we had to do was sit tight for a few more minutes. Sit tight and wait for the fire brigade. Not even Cooper could stop a whole emergency service.

Shelby was curled up on the ground, her eyes tightly shut. The only sign that she was alive was the fluttering motion of her chest as she breathed in and out: shallow, panicky gasps.

'Hey, Hog Girl,' I said. 'Don't sweat it, the fire engine will be here soon.'

'A fire truck?' Shelby opened one eye and looked up at me. 'Can you hear the siren?'

'No,' I admitted, 'but the fire's been going for ages now . . . somebody's bound to have seen it.'

Shelby sat up. 'Lauren, it only started, like, about two minutes ago.'

'Whatever, we'll make it.' I swallowed. My throat was still burning from the fumes I'd inhaled. I pointed to the chair. 'If you stand on that you can get your head through the window. We'll be OK until the fire fighters get here.'

Shelby struggled to her knees and leaned against the chair, her face tipped to the window. Her skin was a deathly grey colour.

'I feel dizzy,' she said.

I reached out my hand to steady her. 'Let me help,' I said.

'Wow.' Shelby turned to me, raising her eyebrows. 'Who'd have thought . . . Nurse Lauren.'

I stared at her. I couldn't figure her expression at all. All of a sudden, words I hadn't even consciously thought spilled out of my mouth.

'You really hate me, don't you?' I said.

I froze. Why on earth had I said that?

Shelby stared at me. Several long seconds passed.

'Yes,' she said.

My stomach shrivelled inside me. Despite the naked honesty of my question, I hadn't really expected Shelby to be honest back.

Resentment rose inside me. Hadn't I just risked my life to save her?

'You've got no reason to hate me,' I said, trying to keep my voice steady. 'I've done nothing to hurt you. *Ever*. In fact, I've gone out of my way to be nice to you.'

Shelby's eyebrows shot up. '*Nice?*' she said with withering scorn. 'If the past two years have been you being *nice* then I'd hate to see what you being mean would look like.'

'What are you talking about?'

'Well, what about what you nearly said yesterday or whenever it was . . . about how you wished I'd been kidnapped instead of Madison.'

Oh, man. 'I *didn't* say that,' I said, my face reddening.

'Yeah, but it's what you were *going* to say.'

'No,' I protested. 'I was just upset. I didn't mean it.'

'No? Like you didn't mean to take Madison away from me . . . or Mom or Dad or—?'

'What?' I said. 'How on *earth* did I take *anyone* away from you?'

'Madison and I were real close until you came back.'

'No, you weren't,' I snapped. 'You were bullying her, for goodness' sake.'

Shelby shrugged. 'That started afterwards, because of *you*. Anyway, with Mom and Dad . . . you were all they ever thought about. All my life it was Martha Lauren this, Martha Lauren that . . . their lives were dominated by whether some old lady in Tampa had seen you or if you'd turned up in some elementary school in Chicago . . . or—'

231

'None of that was my fault.' I folded my arms. 'I didn't *ask* to be kidnapped.'

Shelby sighed. I glanced at the door. Smoke was still seeping into the room, but at least the air in here was relatively breathable.

'Don't you see that you were always there – like this idealised person out in the world somewhere who I had to live up to . . . they never gave me a chance.' Shelby's mouth trembled. 'And once you came back, it got worse. Our whole lives turned upside down. Look at the way Mom and Dad ran off to London to buy that apartment and the way every holiday was dominated by making sure *you* had time with *both* your families. Everyone thought it was all so hard on you having to deal with four parents, but all four of them tiptoed around you like you were a queen. And you acted like one too.'

I opened my mouth to make some cutting remark back about Shelby being pretty good at acting like a queen herself when, without warning, something someone had once said to me came into my head.

You have four parents who love you. For that maybe it is possible to belong in two places.

I bit my lip. I'd never really compared my situation to Shelby's before. I thought of Duchovny. He was her father and he certainly didn't love her.

'It still wasn't my fault that I got taken away when I was a little girl,' I said.

'Maybe *that* wasn't,' she said, 'but afterwards, when you

232

came back, you were so smart and so pretty and I just felt ugly whenever I was next to you.'

I stared at her. Was that really how she'd felt? 'Me coming back didn't change Sam and Annie's feelings for you,' I said.

'Yes, it did.' Shelby sniffed. 'I used to be Mom's favourite, like Madison was Dad's. But once you came back *you* were her favourite.'

'That's not true,' I said, though inside I wasn't so sure. Annie had followed me around everywhere when I came to live with them. It drove me nuts, to be honest. With a jolt, I realised that I'd never once considered just how difficult seeing Annie grasping for my attention must have been for Shelby.

'It is *so* true, Lauren.' Shelby sighed. 'Don't you see? You go in search of a Mom and a Dad who never wanted to lose you and who are over the moon to have you back.' She looked down at the floor and lowered her voice. 'I find out my Mom had an affair and my Dad isn't who I think he is and *my* dad . . . my *birth* dad . . . he doesn't want to know me.' She looked up at me and there was real pain in her eyes. 'I heard him . . . Duchovny . . . talking to Cooper Trent. He said I was a mistake . . . an accident. He doesn't want to have anything to do with me.'

That was true. And in that moment I saw Shelby in a way I'd never seen before. *Her* life dominated by my disappearance. *Her* life thrown into turmoil on my return. She had Annie, for sure, but Sam had died and now she'd discovered another father . . . one who wasn't at all interested in knowing her.

I'd never had to deal with either of those things.

We looked at each other. I wanted to say something . . . something honest and kind.

'Shelby—'

A huge explosion shook the building. The ground trembled under our feet. Shelby screamed. I clutched at the chair beside me.

'What the hell was that?' Shelby gasped.

I struggled onto the chair. 'Come on, get up here,' I ordered.

'But—' Shelby's next words were lost as another explosion, even louder than the first, rocked the building to its core.

I held out my hand to her as the door blew in on us, off its hinges. And a huge ball of fire rushed furiously into the room.

31

Saving Shelby

There was no time to think. Instinctively I hauled myself up through the dormer window so my head and shoulders were outside, my legs tucked up underneath me and all my weight on my arms. I could feel the scorch of the fire on the soles of my feet.

The next few seconds seemed to last an eternity. I knew I couldn't hold my own weight for much longer. I tried to push myself up, higher, so I was properly through the window.

It was no good, my arms were too weak. I slid back into the room, finding the chair below me with my toes. I looked down. What had happened to Shelby?

Fire was now raging inside the room. It was all around the sides, creeping up all four walls, eating at the furniture. Smoke rose above and between the flames. My heart drummed in my ears. In the dim distance a siren was sounding.

'Shelby!' Again my yell came out as a gasp.

'Lauren?' Shelby's head peered out from behind a filing cabinet across the room. She was curled up on the floor. Her face was grimy and her cardigan, still clutched in her hand, was singed. 'Is that a siren outside?'

'Yes,' I said, listening again to the fire engine. It was getting nearer. 'Are you OK?'

Shelby shook her head. 'I tried to roll out of the way,' she gasped, 'but my legs got burned.'

I looked down as she crawled into view. Her jeans were blackened from the knees down. I winced, then jumped down from my chair, onto the ground. The carpet itself was relatively free from fire, but the heat was overwhelming. Smoke filled my ears and nose and mouth, choking me.

I picked my way across the room and reached Shelby. She was trying to push herself up, but the effort was too much. She lay back, coughing uncontrollably.

I looked round. The carpet might be clear, but the fire was still fierce at the sides of the room. The dense smoke was worst of all. It filled my lungs, making it virtually impossible to breathe.

'We have to get onto the roof,' I gasped. 'Then the fire engine will see where we are.'

'I can't move,' Shelby said.

I glanced down at her blackened jeans again.

'My legs hurt,' Shelby whimpered.

'Come on.' I reached under her armpits and tried to haul her upright. The chain, still attached to the grate I'd yanked out of the wall, dangled limply from her wrist.

Flames licked at the walls around us.

I dragged Shelby back towards the window.

'Aaagh,' she moaned.

I peered up at the dark night sky above us. The fire siren sounded close.

'The fire fighters are nearly here,' I said. 'If we both stand on this chair we can get our heads through the window.'

'I can't,' Shelby whispered. 'Can't feel my legs.'

Coughing, I hauled her upright. She was a dead weight in my arms. My muscles ached with the effort, but I forced myself on.

I laid Shelby against the chair while I clambered up and put my head through the window. The air outside was no longer clear, though still blissful to breathe compared to the air in the room. Huge tongues of fire were licking up the side of the building.

Smoke billowed around me, blocking out my view of the sky, but I could hear the siren again and, a moment later, voices shouting. I tried to yell, but my throat was too sore and smoke-swollen. I reached my arms through the window and waved. I could see nothing through the smoke, but maybe, just maybe, one of the fire fighters would see me.

After a moment, I took a deep breath and slipped back into the room below. It was like a picture of hell, with walls of flames – writhing and angry – wherever I looked.

Shelby was still slumped against the chair. She was coughing and sobbing, tears making a track down her grimy cheeks.

'The fire fighters are here.' I grabbed her arm and gave her a shake. My heart was racing, but I was so determined we were going to make it that I wouldn't let myself feel afraid. 'We're going to be OK, Shelby.'

She shook her head and fell into my arms and we hugged.

It was the first time Shelby and I had ever held each other.

I disentangled myself. 'Climb up to the window,' I ordered.

Shelby raised one leg, but as soon as she rested it on the seat of the chair, she screamed with pain.

'OK, OK,' I said, coughing. My lungs felt raw, like someone had got inside me and sprayed me with acid. My breathing was shallow and rasping.

'Go,' Shelby whispered. 'Go and get help.'

I bit my lip. I was certain that as soon as I stopped holding her, Shelby would collapse onto the floor again. On the other hand, I had to make sure the fire fighters knew we were in here.

I lowered her carefully onto the floor and hauled myself onto the chair again. The dizziness I'd felt before was back . . . the blackness at the edge of my vision . . . I raised my head through the open window and waved frantically.

'Help!' I gasped. 'Please, help!'

There, in front of me, rising over the roof in a box attached to an extendable ladder, I saw the fireman. His face was covered by a helmet and he was dressed from head to toe in a brown uniform.

I waved again. He shouted something I couldn't hear.

I slipped back down, into the room. The smoke was denser than ever, clutching at my throat.

Shelby was still slumped against the chair.

I grabbed her arm. 'They're here.' My voice was just a whisper now. I leaned in close to her ear. 'Hang on, Shelby, they're right here.'

Shelby looked round at me. She blinked, then pulled me close so her mouth was right by my ear.

238

'You have to get out of here now,' she whispered.

'Yes,' I said, 'we're *both* getting out.'

'It's got to be you,' Shelby whispered again. 'Mom can't lose you again. And Madison needs you.'

'It's going to be both of us,' I said. 'I promise you.'

And then Shelby looked me in the eye. Her expression was a mix of frustration and defeat – and love. It was a look I'll remember for the rest of my life.

'I shouldn't have said I hate you,' she said. Her voice was so faint I could barely hear her. She coughed and closed her eyes. 'I was mad at you for acting so tough . . . making me feel like a jerk . . . I'm sorry.'

Terror rose up inside me. 'I'm sorry too. I wish—'

'Don't sweat it,' Shelby whispered. She leaned right against me and whispered in my ear. 'Just remember, no-one does it on their own. Not even you.'

I could hear the smile in her voice . . . and then she slumped into my arms. I staggered against the chair, almost knocking it over. The flames were so close now. The smoke filled my head.

'LAUREN?' The shout came from above.

I looked up. A fireman was reaching through the window towards me.

'Give me your hand!' he yelled.

I looked at Shelby. *Take her first*. I tried to haul her up to him, but there was no strength in my arms to lift her. The black was crowding in on me.

'I can't take you both at once!' the fireman yelled. 'Give me your hand. I'll come straight back in for her once I've got you.'

239

I held out my arm. Smoke billowed up around me. Reality seemed to fade around me. Was this what dying felt like?

As I closed my eyes, I felt a strong hand grip my wrist.

With my last ounce of energy, I pushed myself up against the chair. As the fireman hauled me through the window, I let go of Shelby.

32

Eyes Tight Shut

I don't remember much of the next few minutes. I know I was swung through the air and laid against something cold and metallic. The air was still full of smoke. I kept my eyes shut and took shallow breaths through my nose. The next thing I knew I was being loaded onto a trolley – I could hear its wheels squeaking. I was covered with a blanket, and a mask providing sweet fresh air was put over my face. I kept my eyes shut. Where was Shelby? Was she OK?

Voices suddenly surrounded me. Low, soft voices I didn't recognise, talking about burns and IV drips and intubation, whatever that was. And then louder, hysterical voices. Annie and Jam and Madison.

'Where is she?' That was Jam.

Was he talking about me?

I kept my eyes closed. If I kept them shut then Shelby would be all right. *Please*.

The strange low voices were talking calmly.

'They're working on the sister now.'

Did they mean Shelby? I kept my eyes tight shut, praying she was OK.

241

'Lauren?' A small voice, breaking with a sob. A small hand curling round my fingers.

That had to be Madison. I didn't want her to worry. I squeezed her hand tightly, though I still didn't open my eyes.

'She's holding my hand.' Madison's voice rose. 'Lauren?'

I had a sudden flashback to the hospital room where, two years ago, Annie and I had sat on either side of Madison's bed, waiting for a sign that she was alive. After an eternity, Madison had squeezed *my* hand.

For some reason I wanted to point out the irony of this, but the mask over my face made it hard to speak. I lifted my hand, trying to take it off. It was like lifting a heavy metal bar.

'Hey, my love, that's giving you oxygen, leave it for now.' A firm hand pressed the mask back in place.

But what about Shelby?

I couldn't open my eyes until I knew if she was OK because opening them would jinx everything.

I felt the trolley I was on being slid up a ramp. The air around me grew warmer and there was the faint smell of disinfectant. I knew, though my eyes were still shut, that Madison had gone and that I was inside an ambulance.

No. I didn't want to leave here until I knew if Shelby was OK.

Where was Annie? She would know. She would tell me.

I lifted my hand, again trying to push the mask off.

Sister. I tried to speak, but my throat was too swollen and my lips wouldn't obey my command. The word came out as a hiss.

242

'You're going to be fine.' The same calm, male voice who'd spoken before.

Not me. Shelby.

And then I heard the scream rising into the air. Annie's scream. A terrible, raw wail that could only mean one thing.

I held my breath. I kept my eyes shut.

I wouldn't believe it.

There was a shuffling movement beside me. The man – the paramedic – who kept putting the oxygen mask over me was speaking again, but from further away.

I strained to hear what he said. He was talking to another man. Their voices were low and respectful.

'The sister didn't make it.'

The words were as simple and clean as the air I was now breathing. But my mind wouldn't accept them.

And then the paramedic came back and he laid his hand over mine and though he said nothing, the gentleness of his touch told me it was true.

A single hot tear trickled down my cheek. I kept my eyes shut. I might know the truth, but I wasn't going to face it.

The doors of the ambulance slammed shut and the engine started. The siren sounded and I wondered vaguely what it was for, before realising it was for me.

I kept my eyes shut all through the journey and as the trolley I was lying on was bumped out of the ambulance and across uneven ground, into the hospital.

More people fussed over me.

243

'Can you open your eyes, honey?' It was a new voice. A woman. A nurse, I was guessing.

There was a sharp prick in the side of my arm. My heart raced for a second, wondering what I'd been injected with. And then my head swam into unconsciousness.

When I woke, the first thing I was aware of was the tube coming out of my mouth.

And then I remembered Shelby.

The sister didn't make it.

'Lauren?' It was Mum's voice.

My eyes sprang open. She and Dad were sitting beside my bed, their drawn faces almost the same colour as the white walls of the ward.

I took in the room – the empty bed opposite, clean and clinical – then looked back at Mum and Dad. I tried to speak, but the tube in my mouth went right down, into my throat, which felt strangely numb.

'Lauren?' Mum leaned forward, her face creased with anxiety. 'How are you feeling? Can you blink to let me know you're all right?'

I closed my eyes and opened them again.

'One for "yes, I'm all right" . . . d'you think that's what she meant, love?' Mum turned anxiously to Dad.

'Well, ask her,' Dad said.

Mum turned back to me. 'One for "yes, I'm OK apart from my throat and lungs".'

I blinked slowly again.

And then I remembered Shelby again . . . that final look of hers – all hopelessness and love – pushing its way into my mind's eye.

Just remember, no-one does it on their own. Not even you.

'We're hoping they'll take the tube out later today or tomorrow,' Mum said. 'You suffered smoke inhalation, but the doctors say you'll be fine.' She moved still closer.

Dad reached for my hand and gave it a squeeze.

'You might have a sore throat for a while, but they've done a bronchoscopy and some blood tests,' Mum went on, 'and they don't think there's any permanent damage.'

'Provided you don't take up smoking,' Dad said.

He was trying to make a joke, though it came out far too serious. I attempted a smile.

I'm glad you're here.

And I truly was.

I stayed in hospital for two whole days. They took the tube out of my mouth the next morning. It was still hard for me to talk in more than a whisper and the doctors were keen I shouldn't strain my voice, so – apart from Mum and Dad – I was only allowed visitors for a few minutes at a time.

Jam came to see me, full of remorse that he'd left me and Shelby on that second floor. I told him – in a fierce whisper – that he didn't have anything to be sorry for.

I knew, rationally, that Shelby's death was Cooper Trent's fault. He was the one who'd left us in that office building to die. He was the one who'd kidnapped us in the first place.

But somehow I couldn't help feeling that I'd failed her.

A policewoman explained that once Cooper Trent had lured us into the building, he had sneaked up behind Annie and knocked her out so she couldn't raise the alarm. He hadn't needed to kill her, as she couldn't identify him, but he would have almost certainly murdered Madison if he'd found her.

'Your little sister was very brave, hiding from him until the fire engine arrived. He was obviously waiting to make sure the fire took hold, but the sirens scared him off,' the officer said. 'Don't worry, though. We're on his trail.'

Later that day, Annie brought Madison in to see me. Madison chatted away, her big brown eyes round and solemn as she told me how she'd woken up on the back seat of the car to see Cooper attacking Annie and had hidden behind some bins outside a building up the road.

Annie herself said very little. She sat beside me, her hair neatly combed and her clothes properly ironed. But there was a dead look in her eyes that chilled me to the bone.

'Mommy's taking some special pills,' Madison whispered into my ear. 'Because of Shelby.'

And that was the closest anyone came to talking to me about Shelby's death. I guess they didn't want me to have to face it until I was better, but it preyed on my mind the whole time.

Shelby was dead. Gone.

It was too big to believe.

Mum and Dad were at my bedside most of the rest of the time. They sat with me and read to me and chatted about getting me home as soon as possible. On my second day in hospital, they brought me a laptop so I could watch stuff online. Rory even came in for a brief visit to show me a huge model aeroplane he'd made out of cereal packets. I tried to show some interest, but the truth was that the more time passed, the more the pain of losing Shelby built up inside me.

I didn't really understand it. We had never been close. And yet the last few moments we'd shared had made me see Shelby in a completely different light. I'd always thought of her as the selfish one, but now I could see that I'd been selfish too – never really trying to see life from Shelby's point of view at all.

The worst thing was that there was, now, absolutely nothing I could do about it.

The police came to take a statement on the afternoon of the day I got home. Mum hovered anxiously while I told them – my voice still hoarse – how we'd been locked into the first storage room and how, later, I'd dragged Shelby with me to the second.

The police explained that they were close to catching Cooper and, the following day, Mum and Dad brought me the news that he had been killed while resisting arrest and all the money he'd stolen had been recovered, as had the bodies of Frank, Rick and Julianne.

I felt nothing.

I felt nothing about anything.

Even though it had only happened three days ago, Shelby's death seemed to belong to another lifetime. It felt like some horrible dream that I still hadn't properly woken up from. I didn't want to talk to anyone. I didn't want to see anyone, not even Jam.

Mum and Dad were clearly worried about me, but the more time passed the more shut up in my head I felt. And then, one day, about a week after I'd come out of hospital, Jam showed up out of the blue.

'Hey, Lazerbrain,' he said, peeking his head round my bedroom door.

I was sitting propped up on pillows on my bed, staring at a school book. I wasn't reading it, but Mum had, in the last few days, got back to nagging me over my revision so it made life easier to wander around with a relevant book in my hand. I was, as she pointed out, getting behind when it came to my GCSE preparations and the exams were less than two months away.

I didn't care.

I just wanted to be left alone.

'Lauren?' Jam wandered over.

With an effort, I turned my head to look at him.

'What's up?' I said. Perhaps if I had a quick chat he'd leave me alone too.

Jam crossed his arms and frowned.

'Nothing's "*up*",' he said. 'I just wanted to see you.'

'Oh.' I couldn't think what to say. 'That's nice.'

Jam squatted down in front of me. He looked deep into my eyes.

'Shelby dying wasn't our fault,' he said. 'We did the best we could to save her. *You* nearly died, trying to save her.'

I turned my face away, but he reached out and gently turned it back.

'Stop beating yourself up,' he said gently.

'I'm not,' I said. 'I'm fine.'

'Don't lie to me, Lazerbrain.' Jam smiled and, in spite of everything, that smile pierced through the numb fog in my brain.

'I *am* fine,' I protested. But even as I spoke, tears were leaking out of my eyes.

I brushed them away, but more followed and soon I was wailing my guts out.

Jam put his arm round me and let me cry. When I'd finished, he took my face in my hands.

'Don't,' I said, suddenly self-conscious about how puffy and red my eyes must be. I fingered the wooden oval round my neck. 'I look awful.'

'Hideously gorgeous,' he said with a big grin. He pointed to the wooden necklace. 'That's why I gave you that, remember? You're self-obsessed and impulsive and vain and I love you to bits, OK?'

'Well, I hate you,' I sniffed, grinning back. 'Coming into my life and understanding me . . . you're the world's most disgustingly perfect boyfriend and . . . and everything's better when you're with me.'

Jam laughed. 'Are you actually admitting that you need another human being? That you've finally realised you don't have to handle everything by yourself?'

I smiled, remembering what Shelby said just before she died.

'Maybe,' I said, sitting back against my pillows. 'Maybe I am.'

Nobody does it alone. Not even me. And it isn't just Jam I need, either. There's Mum and Dad and Rory. And Annie and Madison. Especially Madison.

I'm going to need all of their help as I face the challenges ahead – coping with a world that suddenly doesn't have Shelby in it . . . my GCSEs and whatever comes after them . . . making it work with Jam when we get into the sixth form . . . and dealing with the fact that Sam isn't my birth father after all – that the man whose genes I carry was some anonymous medical student who doesn't know Madison and I exist. I have no interest in finding out who he is. Not now. Not yet.

Who am I?

There's no one answer to that. We are all becoming ourselves every day – creating a past to take into our future. And other people are the biggest part of what makes us who we are.

Even the ones we thought we hated.

Even when it's too late to change anything, no matter how much we wish we could.

Even though sometimes it isn't until we lose someone that we realise what they gave us – like my sister.

My sister, missing.